Beyond
the *Painting*

Masood Vahdani

PARTRIDGE
A Penguin Random House Company

To order additional copies of this book, contact
Toll Free 800 101 2657 (Singapore)
Toll Free 1 800 81 7340 (Malaysia)
orders.singapore@partridgepublishing.com

www.partridgepublishing.com/singapore

CHAPTER 1

O day of Darkness! What evil spirit moved our minds when for the sake of an earthly kingdom we came to this field of battle ready to kill our own people?

The Bhagavad Gita

Science was Dr Eve Ash's religion. All the sorrows and joys in her life had been driven by a never-ending hunger for knowledge. The right side of her face was burned in May 1982 during an unsuccessful scientific experiment, and ever since, she had worn a special mask made of silver to cover the scar. A rose was carved into the mask to remind her constantly of her past beauty; the road to ugliness travels through beauty, but the road to beauty begins with having faith in one's inner worth.

She was an underdog in the scientific world, and despite her strong ambition, she had produced no results for many years. However, this began to change in July 1985, when finally, she had a breakthrough and was then in demand due to her discovery. Pharmaceutical companies were chasing her like a pack of Turkish wolves chasing a lamb; the difference was, Eve Ash was greedy. She wanted her work to be recognised, and none of those companies wanted her or her work; they wanted her vision. They wanted to engage her in a loveless business affair. A long series of meetings had proven that her silver mask was a far more faithful friend than any of those businessmen in their cookie-cut suits. None of them triggered her sense of curiosity. They were ordinary people. *A suit does not make a beast a real man, but makes a man a real beast*, she thought to herself.

On 20 December 1985, she received a letter at her apartment in Cambridge, a booking confirmation for the Royal Suite in the Hotel Russell, London. There was a small note attached, which read:

> *Dear Dr Ash,*
> *Your work has led to some unexpected and intriguing results.*
> *I would consider it a personal honour if you were to accept my*
> *invitation to London. I dare say that like you, I am a humble*
> *visionary. With your permission I would like to unite my vision*
> *with your own. The result shall alter the course of your research*
> *forever.*
> *Your humble servant,*
> *The Painter*

If this letter had been addressed to someone else, she would have dismissed it or taken it as a practical joke, but for our half-faced scientist, knowing the unknown was another lab test, and this was a journey that must be taken no matter what the consequences. She began to question the letter. Although the confirmation appeared genuine, the note was written by hand, and both the handwriting and the paper were of good quality. 'The Painter' suggested the author was an egoistical man, and the letter's firm but gentle tone indicated that he was not only interested in her work but also her character. At last she felt a sense of recognition and acknowledgement, and decided to spend Christmas in London.

On 21 December Eve sat at the hotel bar, drinking a glass of red Merlot vintage of 1982, the same year as her accident. She was holding the glass in her hand as the beloved holds the soul of a lover, sipping it slowly until finished. She observed the people around her, noticing their mannerisms and interaction. When she had arrived at the hotel earlier that day, there was a note requesting her to be at the hotel bar by 7 p.m. She had decided to wear one of her best outfits: a white shirt, black jacket and long black skirt. For the first time in months, she had let her long blonde hair fall free, like a waterfall of gold chains flowing down her frail shoulders. She wanted to look her best for the meeting with the Painter.

A blend of curiosity, excitement and insecurity brought up the same nagging questions. Who is he? What does he want from me? Why me?

Several people entered the bar; many of them stared at her and of course the mask.

She put her hand on the mask and muttered, 'You silly mask.'

When the clock showed 7 p.m., the door opened and a man entered the bar. He was in his early forties, rather tall and well built. His skin was fair, almost a very pale pink. His eyes were the greyest she had ever seen; his hair was also grey and tied back in a small ponytail. He wore Kashmir black: a black jacket, long black trousers, black shirt, black waistcoat and black caucus hunting boots. On his right index finger he wore a gold ring in which was set a large red ruby.

As Eve scanned the man, he walked towards her with the confidence of a hunter and ceremoniously kowtowed.

In a slow, deep, friendly voice, the stranger said, 'Dr Ash, I am at your service.'

She stood up.

'Thank you for your punctuality, Mr…?'

The man returned her smile, shook her hand and sat down.

'Ma'am,' he said, 'you can call me whatever your heart desires. However, my acquaintances call me the Painter.'

Eve was intrigued by his reply. She sipped her wine and then snapped back into professional mode.

'The Painter it is. What can I do for you?'

The stranger smiled again and asked, 'Aren't you going to offer me a drink?'

Eve suddenly felt embarrassed. 'Oh, I totally forgot. Can I get you anything?'

'May I drink from your glass, or is that too unhygienic for you?'

She liked his straightforward manner. 'My glass belongs to you.'

He drank from the glass and then waited a moment before saying, 'Plato discovered the cave in 380 BC and since then, mankind has made artificial torches to see it. Life is too short to reach the end of that cave. Would you like to see the end?'

Eve stared at the man. 'Are you a businessman or a philosopher, sir?'

'Neither. All I ever wanted from life was a small house with a white candle burning in it. I wanted to share the same bread as my wife and three imaginary daughters, but that was another world. It was taken from me.'

The Painter's voice was sad and melancholic, but the coolness and practicality soon returned to cover his vulnerability. He touched his ring and continued.

'I know who you are, Doctor, and I know all about your discovery. I want to transform it into a weapon and use it for the benefit of one man, and one man only.'

This last comment made Eve feel uneasy. She had always seen herself as a scientist, not a weapon inventor.

'I believe we have different approaches,' she said sharply. 'I will not use my expertise in that way.'

'Hear me out, Eve; feed my greed and I will feed yours. I know you are not after money. And I know you want to know all that is there to know. But, being mortal makes you limited; you die, and you will die with curiosity. I can prevent that. I can give you what you need to reach the end of Plato's cave: time.'

Eve stood up and said firmly, 'I believe it was not a good idea me coming here. I will pack my bags and leave tonight. Thank you for the room, but I'm afraid we cannot work together.'

As she was leaving, she turned round and saw the Painter sitting calmly in the chair. He was holding the wine glass under his nose, smelling its aroma. She walked towards the elevator, pushed the button, entered and ascended. As the elevator door opened and she stepped out into the corridor, she saw the Painter standing next to the door of her room.

'How is living with one kidney?' he said softly.

Eve suddenly lost her temper.

'How dare you? How do you even know about that?'

'You gave your kidney to your ill husband. That is more meaningful than any love poem or chocolate box on Valentine's Day. And once he was cured he romanced your sister. That is worse than any lie. You were hurt by the one person you loved and trusted. I can give you eternal life; I can give you the chance of seeing them and their children suffer in their old age.'

Eve was shocked. *This man is insane*, she thought.

'You need help! Do not come near me,' she said.

He looked directly into her eyes and said, 'I am not mad. I have a vision for a new painting. My dear, you are part of its landscape. Help me to bring my vision to life.'

He moved swiftly towards her, put one hand on her shoulder and with the other quickly removed the silver mask. The face was certainly damaged. *A real hero is destroyed inside and out.* The skin and tissues of Eve's face were gone, exposing the pink-coloured flesh beneath. The Painter kissed the scar and then licked it.

'I need you for your abilities, and I want you so badly for your disfigured face. I think one day I may fall in love with you for all your imperfections.'

After unveiling his deep fascination for her, he held her tightly in his arms and kissed her passionately, their tongues joining.

Then he asked her one last question.

'Will you drink wine from my glass, Eve?'

CHAPTER 2

"The cure for pain is in the pain."

— Rumi

Being a vampire hunter is the most overrated job in the world. You walk around at night, trying to find clues to the vampires' nests. You don't sleep much in the morning either, as what is left of your consciousness is still reliving the events of the night before. After a few months in the field, the novelty of the job is gone. A hunter will be drained, physically and emotionally, members of their family will become strangers and their souls will be addicted to the smell of rotten vampires' ashes.

The first day you join the Guild – the organisation of vampire hunters – no one will explain to you the hardships you will have to endure; no one will tell you how this journey will change you. All the members will welcome you, and talk about the service you are doing for the wider society. They will tell you how you will serve mankind and will be rewarded for all your efforts. It is exactly like becoming a university lecturer: once you are in, you realise others wanted you in so that you would end up poor and insane like them.

Sarah Murphy was an exception among the hunters. Her father was one of the original founders of the Guild. Over the years, she had seen what hunting vampires had cost her father: two divorces, depression, poverty, alcoholism and finally, madness. The last time she saw him, the old man was in a state hospital on the psychiatric ward. He was running naked in the halls, shouting, 'I want a corpse, a fresh young corpse. I want to marry the corpse and have little bastards with it.'

Sarah was not afraid of ending up like her father. The sole reason she had become a member of the Guild was to prove that her father was simply unwell, and had lost his grasp on reality. She wanted with every inch of her being to prove that killing vampires is a justified crusade, not a psychopathic venture. Upon joining the Guild, the very first thing she noticed was the extent of poverty among the hunters. All the money had gone towards building Tartarus, the main building. The security was extremely advanced, with digital cameras scanning your body and identifying whether you are human or vampire. Behind every door were two strong, aggressive guards who would search you and your belongings. The only people exempt from the security check were the twelve administrators of the Guild: six male and six female. Their posts were for life. If a hunter wanted to rise to the status of an administrator, they would need to be or to have … well, nobody really knew.

On 3rd September 2010 at 9 p.m., Sarah finished recording an audio file. She saved the file onto a memory stick and put it inside an amber-coloured envelope. She wrote on the top: *For the eyes of Dr Helsing.*

Then she stood up from her study desk and played with her curly, now white, hair as she began to walk around her untidy house, one pile of books here, another pile there. Crosses made of steel or wood were all around the house; these icons of the past were mementos of her once Catholic faith, rather than a weapon against the vampires. In the evenings she never turned the lights on in her house. The hunters did not walk in darkness because they enjoy it or it reminded them of the darkness of the vampires' souls; they were underpaid and could not afford the luxury of having lights switched on for more than two or three hours every night.

Her mortgage was overdue, but she knew after tonight all this would be over. She would succeed, and the Guild would finally permit her to see FATHER, the main founder of the Guild; no one expected the president of the administrators to be allowed to see him.

She had convinced herself that her findings were too great to be overlooked by FATHER. She imagined how he would hold her and kiss her forehead. She had dreamt about how he would be a substitute for her own insane dead father. One happy image after another merged in her mind. Of course, the alternative was that she would be killed in the line of duty tonight and would no longer be bothered by bank notices on the mortgage. Either way, she would finally be at peace.

By 9.45 p.m. she was in Concerto Coffee on Haymarket Street. She was waiting for the last report from her informant, after which she would be the queen of the Guild. Her fifty-five years of living in small, smelly houses would be over, years of working in a dead-end job would be finished. Her difficult life would be gone and replaced by a happy one.

She liked the location; it was safe from an ambush. The coffee shop was made entirely of glass windows, allowing her to see the outside world and vice versa. There were too many tourists around; vampires would not risk an attack in such a busy location.

She reminded herself of her early days in the Guild and her education. Her teacher had been an old Romanian woman, who would tell her, 'Sarah, vampires do not have the same courage as human beings. They are soulless, heartless cowards. They only attack in dark, narrow lanes.'

She checked the time: five minutes to ten. She was moments away from happiness.

'Next time I come here I will be able to afford a hot meal instead of a plain black coffee,' she whispered to herself.

She looked outside at the people walking on the street. Young boys and girls holding hands reminded those who were separated from their beloved that they did not deserve this; nothing they did would ever be good enough for those who left them.

Then ten o'clock arrived, and all the happy memories faded from Sarah's mind. Instead, the anxious feeling of duty and unconditional service to mankind penetrated her heart. She looked out of the window again, but saw no one and nothing familiar. Her informant had not arrived yet. A group of young teenagers entered the coffee shop. They were speaking in French; visiting students, perhaps. They were very well behaved for a group of young people. Out of habit, Sarah counted them: seven in total, five girls and two boys. Smartly dressed, all were holding a theatre programme for *Mamma Mia*. The theatre, another luxury she could not afford.

While they waited to be seated, one of them walked charmingly but firmly towards Sarah's table and said in a strong French accent, 'May I take the extra chair?'

Sarah smiled and replied politely, 'My apologies; I am waiting for someone.'

The teenage girl returned the smile, bent over Sarah's table and, while brushing her dyed golden hair from her face, said in a perfect English accent, 'A smile hurts more than a dagger, Sarah.'

Sarah understood what the girl meant. She stood up swiftly, pushed the table over and went for her silver pistol. As her hand touched the weapon, the teenager with great force put her own hand on Sarah's; although bony, it was strong enough to control her.

The teenage assassin shouted vehemently, 'In my dreams I have a plan,' and quickly took a razor out of her blue jacket and sliced Sarah's throat.

The blood ejaculated forcefully from her veins, like tears from a lover's eyes. The teenager's face, hands and clothes were all covered in it.

Sarah dropped to the floor; she tried to cover her throat with her hand to stop the bleeding. Customers were screaming and running from the coffee shop. The teenage girl simply sat at another table and finished a discarded piece of cake while Sarah lay dying. The girl's companions gathered round, and in Sarah's last moments she saw their faces. They were motionless, wooden and cruel like ordinary teenagers; they were not vampires.

Sarah was bathing in a pool of her own blood; she finally felt warm. All those years of living in a cold, dysfunctional family were over. All her failures in life were irrelevant now. She was finally becoming one with the darkness, but she was not afraid; it was reassuring, welcoming and, above all, pure and full of opportunities. There was no need to pretend to be nice any more; one could do justice to one's troubled self.

By the time she was dead, the teenagers had set the coffee shop on fire. When the police finally arrived, they were nowhere to be found.

A TV ad announced: 'Describe your personality in three words in your profile, and you will have your dream love partner in less than a month.'

Dr Adam Helsing, resident of Saint Albans, looked at his 60-inch TV and announced his magical three words.

'Retired, alone, lonely.'

He stood up from his cheap sofa and lay down on the floor in front of his TV set.

He brought his legs closer to his belly like a foetus and then repeated, 'Retired, alone, lonely.' Then he shouted, 'Retired, alone, lonely!' He began to snivel.

Adam could not remember how long he had been sobbing, but as the tears ended, the physical pain began. He stood up, turned off the TV, removed his shirt and walked to the bathroom. He turned the lights on and looked at his body. Average; that is, the civilised and politically correct word for saying not too fat. There were scars in the middle of his chest which were not healing properly. He looked at his hair; it was almost white, and very short. He looked at his round face; he remembered what his father had told him once: 'Great men have big faces like yours.' Adam had responded, 'But, father, a bull has a big face as well.' That was the difference between the two Helsings; his father loved his big head, and died with his family and loved ones around him. Adam hated his big head, and so he was always alone and hated by most people, especially the one who meant the most to him: Leto, his daughter.

He picked up a small shaving blade and said with contempt, 'You know what, mother dearest? Let me perfect your creation; it should be your doing, since God or nature wouldn't create anything so imperfect and ugly as me.'

He gave a hysterical laugh and began to mutilate himself. First, he removed a piece of skin from his chest, then pushed the sharp edge of the blade into his flesh.

As the blood began to ooze out, he said, 'I have faith in you, old boy. If I didn't, how could I resent you so deeply?'

A tear fell from his eye. He put the blade to one side and began to punch his 'average' belly until bruises appeared. He looked one more time in the mirror to see what was left of his once promising individualism. The he turned the lights off and went to bed.

At around 2 a.m., the phone rang. At first, Adam didn't pick it up, but whoever it was, was persistent.

Eventually, he answered the phone and said in a grumpy voice, 'Yes?'

A gentle voice on the other end replied, 'It's Christopher, birthday boy.'

'You called me at this hour to say that? Anyway, my birthday was yesterday.'

The man who called himself Christopher answered, 'We need to talk. Please join me in Tartarus as soon as possible. Sarah Murphy is dead ... she has been murdered. She has left you something.'

Helsing scratched his legs in bed and said, 'The next train to London doesn't leave until 5 a.m.'

Christopher gave a childish chuckle and said, 'I have already sent a car to pick you up.'

The phone went dead.

Adam sat up in bed and began to think. He had spoken to Sarah Murphy a few times. He was not interested in her; they weren't lovers, friends or even companions. She was just a hunter, and he had been one of the administrators of the Guild a few years ago.

It was known to everyone that Adam had gone from one woman to another as a young man, just as death goes from one house to another. But age and time had dragged him further into his lonely corner, his books becoming the only things he could trust completely.

While remembering the past, he got out of bed and started to get ready. He was welcoming the idea of the Guild sending him a car; although he had been one of the twelve main members of the Guild, he had never had an office in Tartarus. He was not an office man. He enjoyed the action and the smell of blood.

Tartarus was in an isolated location, 85 miles outside of London; the nearest community was miles away. It had an enormous garden filled with marble statues of the twelve original Greek Titans: Oceanus, Tethys,

Hyperion, Theia, Coeus, Phoebe, Cronus, Rhea, Mnemosyne, Themis, Crius and Iapetus.

Once a visitor had passed through the main iron gates, after a ten-minute walk they would reach the main building, which was designed for two purposes: first, to show the greatness of the Guild for rich Catholics who were investing their money in the vampire hunting crusade, and second, to create a feeling of awe for new hunters so they became absorbed by the ideas of FATHER sooner rather than later. He was never in Tartarus; no one knew where he was except Christopher, the director of administrators, who had held the office since the Guild was created in the late 1960s. Many things were going wrong at that time. Children had finally broken free from their families and wanted to live by themselves, and of course the panic started, with reports of vampire attacks. The reports were soon hushed; the government blamed it on the media and saw it as a rumour speared by the Rock 'n Roll culture and free-spirited young people. Tartarus was built amidst all the fuss, far away from everybody's attention. FATHER did not give much money to his children, the vampire hunters, and spent it on his glory, his Tartarus.

When Adam's car arrived in front of the tall gates, it had already started to rain. He watched it through the car window and wondered for a moment if one day the rain would wash him away, this meaningless little worm, from the surface of the planet.

The facade of the building was made from 500-year-old stones stolen from the ruins of the Incas' temples in Peru. On the pinnacle was a tall bronze statue of Hyades, while on the top of the enemy's house was a fallen Olympian, holding a mask of Zeus in front of his face.

Since Adam was no longer working as an administrator, he was supposed to have a security check; however, the guards allowed him to pass without one, as they knew him quite well, having been hired by him years before.

The long, dark ancient halls of Tartarus were the only location that provided Adam Helsing with any form of respect.

Walking up and down the winding staircases reminded Adam of the magnificent beauty and strength of the place. No force would ever destroy this monument of human madness.

He reached the top level and was directed to Christopher's office. As usual, the room held the sweet scent of roses, which Adam detested.

Christopher was sitting behind his majestic desk.

He looked at Adam and said, 'Thank you, my friend; if only there were ten men like you, I could die a happy man.'

Adam sat on a leather armchair in front of Christopher's desk and ran his hand through his short silver hair.

'I'm just a retired citizen.'

Christopher smiled, playing with his thick moustache.

'You are not retired, you just stopped fighting evil. Welcome back.'

'Welcome back to what?' Adam replied in a melancholic tone.

Christopher stood up and walked towards the coffee table next to his desk. He poured some whisky into a couple of glasses, added a dash of water and handed one glass to Adam.

'You and I always drink the strong stuff. We are strong; that is why we became administrators.'

Adam looked at his own reflection in the whisky; it seemed as if he was swimming and drowning in the void of the brown liquid.

'We were educated people,' he said. 'FATHER wanted university people. That is why we did all we did. It has nothing to do with our strengths; we are not strong at all. We are weak, damaged individuals.'

Christopher smiled, drank some of his whisky and sat back in his chair.

'Good old Adam. Anthropologist and a philosopher; you haven't changed. How FATHER was right.'

Adam was taken aback, but controlled his inner surprise.

'What do you mean?'

'A big incident has occurred, which may change things forever. FATHER wants you and only you on the job. Sarah Murphy might have been a neurotic, strange person, but she gave us a great chance to wipe out all the vampires.'

Adam looked at him seriously. 'And?'

'About two months ago she had a meeting with me. Similar to all the other hunters, she was complaining about her income. In the end, she asked if it was true that once a hunter makes a great contribution to the Guild, he or she can see FATHER. I told her that was correct. I also added that although this is the law of the Guild, it has never happened because no contribution has been good enough for him. Suddenly, she began to jump up and down in the very armchair you are sitting in. She said that she had found a map that could take us to the lair of the leader of the vampires. Naturally, I was not surprised to hear that; I have been in this job forever, and every single low-life hunter has claimed this at least once. She told me that she had firm evidence and that she would soon give it to me. I didn't hear anything for two months, and then four days ago, she was murdered in London, in the centre of the city in front of thousands of people, her throat sliced open like a watermelon.'

'Vampires?'

Christopher smiled cynically. 'No, not this time. They were teenagers; the police haven't found them yet. The coffee shop where she was murdered was burnt to the ground. And all the CCTV cameras in that area stopped working for two hours, including the time the murder happened; we are talking thousands of cameras. The conclusion is that perhaps she was close to something big, and someone, including the bloodsuckers, wanted it for themselves. They probably found some psycho teenagers to do the dirty job for them and that's that.'

Adam stood up, put his empty glass on Christopher's desk and began to walk around the massive office in a circle. After a minute of reflection, he put his hands over his face.

'For over thirty years we have fought these creatures and we have killed thousands of them, yet we never killed any of them that we can call VIP. There is no rank among them, at least not as far as we know. FATHER has told you that there is a leader among them. Okay, let's say there is a king, or a general, or someone of high authority. We don't know why this person would be interested in Sarah's discovery, whatever it was. I think if there is anything to all of this, you and I just had a drink before the war.'

Christopher felt at ease after Adam's short speech, and started to clap his hands.

'Really, Adam, you deserve to be one of the administrators. That's the key word, war; the mother of all art and sciences. Now, she left you a memory stick. Hunters had gone through her house before the police got there; we didn't want one of our members ending up in a tabloid newspaper. *Crazy woman chasing vampires*, they would say. So we wiped the house of any evidence that would refer to vampires, and in the process we found this memory stick addressed to you.'

Adam said calmly, 'Save me the hassle; what was on it?'

'You need to hear it for yourself.'

'Then leave it with me.'

Christopher took the memory stick out of his navy-blue jacket and put it next to a notebook and a pair of small headphones on his desk; then he opened the door and left Adam alone with the final words of a woman who was now part of the void.

CHAPTER 3

"Why is a raven like a writing-desk? Have you guessed the riddle yet?" the Hatter said, turning to Alice again. "No, I give up," Alice replied. "What's the answer?" "I haven't the slightest idea," said the Hatter.

Lewis Carroll

Sarah began to narrate in her sad, nasal voice.

'Hi Adam, how are you? Long time no see, eh? Isn't it sad and ironic to see what's become of us all? I mean, you and I were the future of society, remember? At university our teachers used to say that to us. And you were always the one who would be known as the 'pessimist', weren't you? I remember your famous quote: As children we are the future, as adults we are all lost, as old men we are nothing but irrelevant dark dots of history. The truth is, you were not the wrong prophet. All that could have gone wrong went wrong. You never end up with the people or situations you wanted to end up with. My story is more tragic: I ended up with the only person I wanted to be with, my husband. He was that icy fire that hell had to offer to my life. All these years, these long, wasted years, I wonder how my life would have been if I had married a different person.

'All my life I worked hard to provide for my son and me; I mostly failed to do so. In my job, also, I see myself as a failure. I have killed vampires, and lots of them. But somehow, I never felt close to success. Their existence had become a way for me to forget the mundane aspects of my life; basically everything in this life was dull. I admit I am a coward and therefore I am unable to terminate my existence; instead, I terminate that of others. Yes, I see vampires as people. In fact, they deserve the title of *human* more than any of us. The other day I was shopping at a local supermarket. I saw an ugly old man wearing his house pyjamas, buying all the candies and fizzy drinks he could get. The sight of him nauseated me; he was filthy, and you could smell shit and piss on him; sweat was his perfume. Then he was criticising the government. Why did we give rights to these sub-humans when they don't even take care of themselves, let alone accept their responsibilities in society? Vampires are far more superior. Have you noticed these days that all the bloodsuckers we have killed were artists, highly paid prostitutes, scientists, writers, thinkers, and so on? I have never heard of any hunter that has killed a vampire that wasn't a useful member of society.

'However, I think it's too late for us to embrace the so-called darkness of vampires; we don't have their courage, and we cannot admit that useless people are unnecessary for society. Also, like you and other hunters, I am a hypocrite. I need the money that killing vampires gives me. I need … in fact I beg for FATHER's affection and attention. Christopher told me when one is in the FATHER's presence, one will forget all one's pains and become a true believer. Of course, he has a big purse as well. I don't mind helping myself from it once before it is too late.

'A long time ago, I came to the understanding that human relations were defined by the number 7. Give me a name, and I am almost seven people away from that person. But, this is not the case with vampires. For them, the magic number is 2. We never had to kill more than two vampires at once. There is something fishy about this. Someone must have manipulated the rules of physics for these people, and this someone must also operate from an organization. If we have a Guild, they must have one too.

'I have been looking for a clue for so long, but nothing. For years I searched for an understanding of what happens when they drink our blood. Why do they never attack hunters? I chased the ball, like a lost cat in a narrow alley in Tokyo. For years I searched, until a few weeks ago when I met someone; it was pure luck. There was a brief fight, but I won. Before I could kill her, she begged me to help her become human again. There was something about her that made me curious. To begin with she was the very first vampire I had met who begged for change. Those who are privileged with eternal life have no desire for the mortal one.

'She was different; I felt I could trust her. She was ready to offer as much information as she could. In exchange, she wanted our advanced medical treatments to transform her back to a human state. Our advanced medicine! I laughed in my heart when I heard that. I mean, the Guild's doctors are as good as state doctors. They never cure your illness; our entire health system is a badly written satire. That is why, when you want to get well, you need to pay for a private doctor. Anyway, I shouldn't drift. I made false promises to her and asked Christopher to meet her. He refused; he said it was probably a hoax. So I began to work on her by myself. She didn't know who was in charge of the vampires, but she knew that there was someone. She also spoke of a map, which requires putting two gems together: a sapphire and an emerald. Now, she didn't know which direction this map would lead her, and I trusted her on that. As I am recording this for you, it is a few hours before I meet with her. She phoned me and told me that she had found something about the location of the first gem; she believed a vampire must have it. She did not provide me with any name.

'I am recording this for you because, for the first time in my life, I am scared of the unknown. What if something goes wrong and I die of a heart attack? What if she is killed by other vampires and they hunt me down? What if…? I need you on this; believe me, I know. You are far too damaged to believe in facts and hard evidence. You had to survive on your instinct and hatred for the truth; you lived on a myth for long enough to transform that myth to truth. This vampire girl is for real; I know it, I feel it. If you ever hear this, remember one thing: you are not a pompous, obnoxious idiot like Christopher. You were born free of those human traits. You are fallen, but you brought yourself down. No one can ever damage you except you. And no one can lead you to a great ending but you.'

*

Her voice faded away like all of her actions, or those of anybody else. Rain was brushing the windows of Christopher's office.

'Well, what is the conclusion?' Christopher asked as he entered.

'You are a pompous, obnoxious idiot.'

Christopher began to chuckle. 'I think she may be onto something. Of course, at first I didn't buy her story, but recently she provided us with a great clue, a clue that made me suspect that she may be right after all.'

'What clue?' Adam asked.

'Her bleeding throat,' Christopher said unsympathetically.

Adam touched his own throat and applied a slight pressure.

'Well, you're right about that,' he said. 'She sounded too ambitious, but, like you, I think she may have been up to something. I mean, everything she said about vampires not attacking us was correct. I remember a few years back, this crazy Japanese chemist made small purple balls that were supposed to explode and kill ten vampires. We never used them, not because we didn't want to, but because there was no need. On my busiest night I fought two vampires at most.'

'FATHER knows all about this. We talked together at length; he was here,' Christopher said.

For the first time in years, Adam was amazed.

'FATHER? Here?'

'Yes. FATHER. Here. We talked, and he wanted you in. He knows that you do things efficiently and quickly. He also permitted me to answer your questions … well, some of them.'

Adam paused for a few seconds.

'I won't ask you how FATHER is, or where he currently lives. You will not tell me anyway. I have only one question. What does he think about vampires having an organisation?'

Christopher replied in a firm and confident voice, 'He doesn't think they are organised, he *knows* they are. You see, Adam, for the last ten years there have been many secret operations organised by Tartarus to discover the extent of this vampire organisation. We found nothing; that's why when Sarah came to me with her discovery, I told her she was mistaken. I knew she may have had a clue, but I needed to wait for her to come back with some result. If it was a serious matter, then it should have been handed over to FATHER. You know the rule: the credit of important discoveries always goes to FATHER.'

'Come on, there must be another reason.'

Christopher gave a faint smile. 'Well, FATHER thinks that if we don't move fast enough there will be an open war. The vampires knew that Sarah was coming for them, I'm pretty sure of that. Vampires, we believe, want this war.'

'She spoke of two gems, right? If these gems exist, they will be hidden in different places. If we find the first one and the person who has allocated the gems, we will find out what all the fuss is about.'

'I know. I discussed this with FATHER; it is a risk that we need to take. I mean, we need to find these gems one way or another. Adam, Tartarus is financially on its knees. My friend, our greatness, like our youth, disappeared a long time ago and sadly, these days we hardly have any new recruits. All these gothic clubs, these cults, these social gatherings for discussing vampire literature have taken the young people away. They don't understand the depth of the human ideals we promote any more.'

Perhaps it was because we were blind to how wrong those ideas were, Adam thought.

'I'll see what I can do,' he announced. 'But I want to choose my own team.'

'Thank you, old friend. You can have whoever you like. Tartarus' best hunters are at your service.'

'Your best is not good enough for me. I want one person by my side and one person only: Sarah Murphy's son.'

Christopher would have felt less angry if he had found out his own children had become bloodsuckers.

'No! No way; not him!' he screamed.

Adam smiled calmly. 'He has been in Afghanistan and Iraq for a long time. He has changed, I'm sure of it. Plus, he has the same feelings about his mother as I do about mine. We would work perfectly together.'

'But, you hated your mother,' Christopher said, surprised.

'The old bat is still alive. God keeps postponing meeting her because he knows that she will nag him about being imperfect.'

Then, without shaking Christopher's hand, Adam left the room.

As his car drove him away from Tartarus, the pain in his chest faded, but the pain in his soul was growing stronger than ever.

*

Atakan means having one's ancestors' blood. This can be a great name, since it suggests that one is part of an ancient noble dynasty. It means that one has lived life to the fullest, and that one's efforts are recognised by others. It means that one is bound to be a powerful and connected individual. It means one is a demigod who can open every door anywhere. It means that one can make fun of anybody, yet they are happy that your grace has made fun of them.

All these images aside, Atakan means you will suffer from an ancient incurable illness, delusion; the only tangible legacy our fathers left us from one generation to another. We laugh to mask the pain in our hearts; we smile to mask the tears of our souls. We celebrate to make a masquerade of our failed lives.

Sergeant Atakan Murphy was not deluded about his name or his position in life. However, this did not stop him finding the path to happiness. But his enlightenment was followed by depression; he started to see things, not when he was under the fires of hell raised by Shiite terrorists in Iraq, but when he was eating a Deluxe Macdonald burger in London. There were young people everywhere and they were happy. He felt happy for them. But then suddenly, a fight broke out among these happy youngsters and they were at each other's throats. Atakan thought if they had guns and were following a clergyman, they would have the power to incarnate Basra in London.

Sarah had always told him about his forefathers, how they were of noble blood and linked to the Ottoman Empire a long time ago. As a teenager he felt proud of having such a background. But as he grew older, he realised the curse; that his genes were damaged for good. He read history books and realised the great services of his ancestors to the world; like any other kingdom on the planet, their actions can be summarised in three words: Destruction of Others.

After reading hundreds, maybe even thousands of books, Atakan realised that he could not be an ordinary person; he simply could not become one of the happy people. He would be unable to enjoy the bliss of delusion, and was condemned to be different and suffer for it. That was when he began to hate his mother. Naturally he would hate his father, but he had been out of the family portrait for many years. Deep down, he knew his mother was a good sort and he knew for sure that she would die to make him happy. But this made him loathe her all the more.

Adam Helsing recruited Atakan for the Guild. For Sarah's son, Tartarus was paradise. He would chat with the hunters, walk through the corridors and feel like an ancient commander. He killed his first vampire when he was 17 years old. That same night, he lost his virginity to a prostitute. Vampires and whores were God's finest creatures, and made a troubled boy a soulless adult.

As he grew older, he became more and more estranged from his mother. By the time he turned 21, he wouldn't even mention to other people that he had a mother. And the more he hated her and thus his own feminine side, the more he became lost in his hatred for vampires and began to feel sexually aroused while killing them. This continued for a while, until the Guild started to feel worried and decided to commence an investigation. After killing them, Adam would remove their fangs and hide them. Eleven out of twelve administrators wanted him expelled. Adam Helsing was the only man who didn't have a problem with Atakan's attitude, but he represented a single vote, a vote that died among the protests of the majority. When Atakan left the Guild, so did Adam. Atakan was one of only two people Adam could possibly love.

After joining the army, the young hunter felt more and more angry. The level of humanity shown by the army was too much; he would see every man, woman and child on the streets of Herat and Basra as an angel of death. He wanted to kill them all, but he was not allowed due to the army's rules; his superiors were too noble and good natured for his sadistic desires. His attitude got him fired from the army, and he returned to England at the age of 26. No one but Adam heard anything more about him. For six years, every now and then a letter would be delivered to Adam's house; in fact, Atakan was the only man who ever wrote to the old vampire hunter. But none of his letters made any sense; they were the gibberish of a psychopath.

However, a year before Sarah Murphy was assassinated, there was a change of tone in Atakan's letters, and he began to talk about having remorse for treating his mother badly. He wrote about how even our worst nightmares can help us. He was showing signs of a long-lost gentle soul, sorry for not being a disciplined soldier. Adam took no notice of this new Atakan; he wanted him mean and cruel, and that is why he needed him now. The case that had been offered to the old man was a great chance to resurrect the former Atakan.

Adam did not care for any gems or revelations. He had missed the adventure and hurting others. He had hurt himself a lot for over three decades. Sadly, his body had grown older and weaker, and he couldn't tolerate the physical and emotional pain as well as before. Over the years, because of self-abuse, his nerves were badly damaged, and cold weather, warm weather, anger and hunger would make them even more painful. He needed new bodies to hurt, and vampires were the ideal choice.

One of the last times that Atakan had written to Adam, he had spoken of a cemetery which he called *My cradle of peace and happiness*. He spoke of the many happy hours he had *lived* there, and how he would bribe the old caretaker of this gothic cemetery to walk around the graves late at night. In his last letter, he had written the following:

Greetings,
As I walk among these graves, I come closer to the idea of self-
awareness. I must admit, I am a jealous man. I am suffering
from this trait, for I cannot be like Elizabeth Greene; she is a
friend. She is 32 years old, married with six daughters. I am
not jealous because she has a family and I don't. I'm jealous
because she is dead, and here it says on her grave that she is
remembered by her husband and six daughters. Her date of
death is 3 December 1885. Still, she survived death because

she had loved ones. What about me? That is the question. I will not survive death like her. Where are my loved ones? That is why I have become obsessed with her grave. There is a broken cross on top of it, and on the tombstone there is an angel with little wings. The angel is smiling. I wish I was that lifeless angel and could offer such a beautiful, sombre smile to the visitors.
P.S. Have you seen the prices of video games? They are ridiculously expensive.
Atakan

The young vampire hunter was not his old self any more; through his pain, he had become human.

*

Atakan's entrance into the cemetery was like Moses walking towards God's burning bush; the only difference was that Moses was experiencing self-evaluation and growth, whilst Atakan was set on the mission of self-recreation and loneliness.

The young hunter opened the short iron gate of the cemetery and entered the arena of the dead. He was wearing a pair of jeans, a white hoodie and a pair of muddy white tennis shoes. He put his small backpack on the ground, erected his long body and gazed upon the graves. The night was pitch-black and pleasantly wet. Dark, powerful clouds were marching proudly and majestically through the sky. Atakan looked at them and smiled faintly. He took a small hammer out of his pocket and moved to an old grave. He hammered down part of the tombstone and picked up the broken pieces, which he crushed as much as he could in his hand; then, he took a white tissue from his trouser pocket, which contained two white vampire fangs. The fangs were smashed and mixed with the cemetery powder. The ex-soldier inhaled his self-made drug.

A few seconds later, the kick of the century began. At first, a shiver went through his body, followed by sweating off all the sadness of his past. Finally, he lost his total being to the cemetery. Atakan now saw his red blood cells in front of his eyes; they were dancing seductively, calling his name lustfully. He picked one of the cells and put it in his mouth. He continued with this sweet hallucination, grasping the empty air, thinking it was his own blood.

He heard a noise; something or someone was moving. He turned in the direction of where he thought the sound was coming from.

'Mom, is that you?'

From behind one of the graves came a skeleton, wearing a long black jacket and a bowler hat, both of which were ancient and shabby. The skeleton walked swiftly towards him; once he was face to face with the young man, the skeleton raised his bony index finger and thrust it upon the young hunter's lips.

Then, in a harsh, sarcastic voice, he said, 'Mom? How dare you, old fellow? Isn't it a pity you say that ugly name?'

Atakan stepped back and began to talk to the dead.

'I love her. I just … I just don't like her. Maestro, I wanted to be a good son, but she never let me be one.'

The skeleton that Atakan called Maestro jumped up in the air and kicked his two feet together; the union of the bony feet created an annoying clicking noise.

Once Maestro was back on the ground, he announced, 'My apologies. I died of tuberculosis about 200 hundred years ago; the cough has stuck with me. Now, I hear your problem, and I guess we are in the same boat. We want to be different to who we are, but we cannot perform that miracle. You see, I want to be bad, but I can't. Instead, I am just a funny jerk.'

He took out an old Bohemian violin from his long jacket; maggots were crawling over the instrument and he shook it as hard as possible. A half-chewed finger and hundreds of the yellow stinky maggots fell to the ground.

The classical musician waved the cleansed violin in the air before placing it properly on his arm.

'Ladies and gentlemen,' he shouted, 'let us dance. The night is long, eternity is longer, and if there is a God, hell's whorehouses are ready to entertain us. Now, I must play this beautiful piece on a proper church organ. But hey, my violin should be good enough; the poor souls are already dead anyway.'

He began to play *Toccata* from *Suite Gothique*. As the music progressed, the entire cemetery came to life and the dead rose from their graves. There were all kinds of skeletons: fat, thin, male, female, old, young, even dogs. However, there was one particular skeleton that grabbed Atakan's attention. It belonged to a young girl, perhaps around 4 or 5 years old, who was totally lost among the other skeletons. Her small skull dropped to the ground, and she bent over and picked it up.

Then she began to scream, crying out, 'Mommy? Daddy? Where are you? I'm scared.'

Maestro stopped playing.

'Oh dear, a little girl has lost her mommy and daddy. Imagine being in her position; alone, scared, cold, hungry. Oh well, why bother ourselves? Her life is ruined anyway.'

He was about to continue his music afresh when a large piece of rock hit him in the head, leaving a long crack in his skull.

Atakan and the skeletons looked at the trajectory of the rock, and they saw that the skeleton who had thrown it still had some flesh left on her body. She was wearing a dark green skirt and a black leather coat, and was holding a saxophone in her left hand and another big rock in her right.

While playing with the rock, she said, 'My parents lost me when I was alive. They said I was not decent enough. It was the '70s.'

She pointed to the little girl and said, 'Come here little one. We will take care of each other. We have both been abandoned by our loved ones.'

The little girl moved towards her and hugged the free-spirited corpse. Her new friend looked at her.

'Uhh, your skull is muddy. Let me clean it.'

Then she brought her skirt up and began to wipe the girl's skull.

Maestro came closer and said in a mocking voice to the free-spirited corpse, 'What killed you? Suicide, I bet.'

The corpse looked at him. 'No, it was an overdose. Like I said, it was the '70s.'

'Well, you rebels did not have our class. I mean, listen to your music.'

The Saxophone girl laughed loudly at this last comment and looked round at everyone.

'Did you know *His Majesty* has never played at any major concert? Did you know that when he was alive, no one called him Maestro? Did you know that his wife was happy when he died? Did you know that no one really loved him?'

Suddenly, a skeleton of an old woman who used to be a preacher's wife in the seventeenth century collapsed from shock after hearing the 'L' word.

Maestro started to sweat, and shouted, 'These are, uhh, these are cheap accusations. I was a good musician … sort of. I mean, I could have been good if … if, uhhh, if I had better instruments. And my wife, she … she loved me. She never cheated on me with the local butcher. No, no, it was not her, it was her twin sister. Mind you, when I think about it, I never knew she had a twin sister until now.'

'Shut up!' said a young couple.

As the husband took the ring off his bony finger, he added, 'We died in a fire during our wedding. We never danced properly.'

The free-spirited corpse told them, 'Dance, you shall. It will be better than what we have been discussing.'

Meanwhile, Maestro had crawled back to a corner and was sobbing.

'Oh, Jimmy,' he said, 'you were such a tender goat. I should have married you, not that beautiful blonde.'

The '70s girl dropped the stone and went over to the dead musician.

'Hey, old man, come on, all of us are dead. Even this half-dead friend of yours,' she said, pointing to Atakan. 'I have found a new friend tonight, this little girl. The two of us are happy; your friend is happy too, and high. And the government hasn't yet suggested a law that would make dead people pay taxes for being happy. So let's pretend we *are* happy, since no one can really be happy in this world.'

And so it all began. All the corpses took a musical instrument out of their garments; even the little girl took a little flute out of her pocket. They all began to play a cheerful piece of music; Atakan couldn't remember if he had heard it before. Whatever it was about that music, it gave him the energy to do something. He began to remove all his clothes violently and threw each item in a different direction. Soon, he was dancing among the skeletons of the past, naked, honest and vulnerable. He kissed each imagination of his past life, one by one. The young hunter then relaxed his body of all intensities of the traumas he had experienced in the past; he was dancing naked and happily among the graves. His nudity had stripped him of all concepts of shame, honour, integrity, self-respect and, above all, obsession. The more he danced, the more the images of vampires, corpses and blood escaped his mind. The more he danced, the less he hated his mother. The more he danced, the closer he came to the end of the cave. He was almost there; a warm, cosy environment where he could finally be pure, innocent and free of pain. A warmth that could fool him into feeling a sheer sense of happiness. However, all this would be impossible. Like all human beings, he had no chance of reaching the true, genuine, mature level of happiness he sought.

A hand brought him out of his happy dreams. It belonged to Adam Helsing, the old hunter. He was slapping Atakan's face, and kicking his naked body in the muddy cemetery. The first rule of being happy was that in order to achieve happiness, one must make many other people unhappy. This is not usually true; it is *always* true.

CHAPTER 4

Atakan was lying naked on the ground, covered in the cemetery's mud and dirt.

Adam's eyes were fixated on him. The old hunter was observing what had become of his former pupil. The young hunter's dirty body resembled that of a newborn baby; both had gone on a journey prior to their birth.

Atakan stood up and gazed in amazement at the sun. He brought his hand in front of it and let the bright-yellow rays pass his fingers. A melancholic smile spread over his face.

'Everything looks beautiful in the sunlight. Good to see you, old friend.'

'Hey, your mother is dead,' Adam said emotionlessly.

The former said with no affection, 'I know. I know all the details; good riddance.'

Adam gave a vicious smile. 'Come, you need to wash. I have brought a few bottles of water and some clean clothes in my car. I thought you would be dirty wherever you were.'

As the two men passed the graves, Atakan looked at this dreamland and its peaceful silence. The cold dirt of the grave is the only remedy for a broken heart; it is the only remedy for a tormented soul. The light of the sun was flickering graciously and flirtatiously, like a maiden, among the graves. Atakan knew that the little girl was sleeping in peace. If only he could share her solace. How freeing that would be! Atakan washed himself as much as possible with the water that Adam gave him. A bit of dry mud was stuck to his bald head, but he took no notice. Adam handed him the fresh clothes. As the young man was putting them on, an elderly lady – one of those rare species that are about to be extinct once and for all from our society – and her ugly poodle walked past their car. Like mistress, like dog; the creature and her owner looked at the two men in disgust. One man was putting on some clothes while the other gazed at the young man's naked flesh.

Atakan chuckled and shouted loudly at the old woman, 'Hey, love, how does it feel to be middle class? How does it feel to be the grandmother of a schoolteacher?'

'Shut up, you idiot!' Adam said. 'Get in the car. What is wrong with you? She's just some old woman. Let it go.'

Atakan finally finished getting dressed and hopped in the car.

As Adam sat next to him, the young man said, 'Thanks for asking how I am. Recently, I have become a funny person. Not good funny, but sombre funny. Like a clown who has been too long in the business of being, you know, a clown. Times have changed; jokes have changed. But Mr Clown is not happy any more. Hey, have you seen this?'

He pointed to a tattoo on the palm of his right hand. It was written in *kanji*.

'It reads *Aku*. That's Japanese for evil.'

Adam took no notice and began to drive off. He wondered what had happened to the boy. He used to be reckless, heartless and dark, but now he was like a childish caricature of his old self. Now he was just plain silly, like a condemned aristocrat in the streets of Paris in the 1790s walking towards the scaffold; the man knew he was dead anyway.

'What are you crying about? Let's have a good laugh at the hour of the dead.'

There was no doubt that Atakan had changed. Whatever happened in the war had taken him out of the man-made hell that Adam loved to live in. By becoming a sad clown, the young man had become more human.

'We are going to your mom's house,' said Adam.

'Your answer is wrong. Maggie, my mother, her house is not where you want to go.'

Adam diverted the car swiftly away from the main road and came to a stop.

'Have you gone totally cuckoo?' he asked in amazement. 'What is wrong with you? Who the hell is Maggie?'

Atakan began to talk softly in a feminine voice. 'Why, daddy?' And then in a very deep, hoarse voice he said, 'Are you afraid of a strong, independent woman?'

Adam stared at him, not knowing what he was talking about.

'Dear Lord! You are more insane than usual. Tell me, boy, what are you saying?'

'Insanity, old friend, is the milk I have drunk from the bosom of life. Now, if you are looking for some secret clue to Sarah's things, don't waste your time by going to her house. There won't be anything … exciting there. In fact, there was never anything exciting there. But, if we go to my aunt's house, some of Sarah's stuff will be there. It was Sarah's workshop, so to speak.'

'I never knew she had a sister.'

'She has been dead for a long time now.'

The old hunter asked for directions to the house and then put the postcode into the car's GPS. During the journey, which took them through extensive countryside, Adam thought about what Atakan had said. Maybe he was afraid of strong women. Maybe he avoided them and found comfort in weaker members of the opposite sex. Maybe he was insecure about his own strength. Maybe his dominating mother had killed off all the masculinity in his character.

By the time they reached the house, as always Adam had managed to repress all the doubts and questions in his heart. That's the only outcome of being angry – one dose not reflect on one's own weaknesses.

Atakan was the first to jump out of the car.

'Sarah was looking after the house. She always complained she had no money, yet she never sold it. Let's break in.'

The house was one of those typical modern country houses in England; lovely to look at in a catalogue, but boring to live in. Atakan picked up an old key hidden under an empty flower pot outside and unlocked the front door. The two hunters entered.

The interior was like being inside the mind of an artist; many great and beautiful things, but no discipline at all.

'Why the hell have the police not come here before?'

'My aunt changed her family name years ago,' Atakan explained. 'No one but me knows that Sarah used to come here. This is a castle compared to her house.'

Adam agreed with the latter point. This house was much more spacious than Sarah's South East London residence. However, one could see that the same person had lived in both places. Newspapers were everywhere, and there were different maps from different historical periods of England covering the walls and floor, of the Ottoman Empire, ancient Egypt and medieval Korea, amongst others. On the old green shabby and torn sofa in the living room lay a small diary. It was open.

The old man picked it up and recognised Sarah's handwriting. She had written down questions such as: Where do they earn money? Can they make babies? What is the Ark? Adam was not puzzled by this; he had seen Sarah holding the diary many times.

Among the numerous questions written on the page, the one that particularly intrigued Adam was *What is the Ark?*

The house had three large rooms and a small attic. As they went from one room to another, Atakan carefully looked for something, going through closets, bookcases, suitcases and desk shelves. Then he cursed his luck.

Adam let him be and went up the staircase to the attic, where he found a dusty old bed. He sat down on it and looked at the diary again.

'The Ark,' he whispered.

As Adam was daydreaming what the Ark could be, Atakan entered the attic holding a small toaster.

'Here, I think I've found it.'

Adam put the diary in his pocket.

'What? Are we going to eat toast and jam?'

The young man laughed hysterically. 'Did you know that Judas believed the other apostles were jealous of him, for he was the dearest and nearest to the Lord? If we had faith in this version of history, then the crucifixion would be nothing more than man-made fiction.'

He started to jump up and down while still holding the toaster in his hand.

'The Lord is great and his jokes are cruel and his love is conditional and I am but a frustrated, angry little nobody,' he shouted, and then threw the toaster at the wall.

The toaster was broken, but Atakan picked it up and began to smash it further by punching the metal as powerfully as possible with his fist.

Adam watched with surprise and confusion. Was it possible that the boy who had once been his protégé had lost his mind and become crazy?

The old hunter tried to calm the angry young ex-soldier down, but the latter kept fighting the toaster until his hands were covered in blood.

When he finally stopped, Adam looked at him.

'Now, what the hell was that performance for?'

'Uh, we, uh, uh, have a winner.'

He produced an expensive, well-designed and phosphoric amber-coloured visitor's card.

Adam took it with delight.

'How did you know this was in the toaster?'

Atakan sat on the floor and said mockingly, 'Well, she used to hide things that were of great importance in there, including a photo of me in a medieval costume when I was 10 or 11 years old. The day she took that photo, she had taken me to one of those theme parks. That day we … we were happy. You know, we were happy together and we were happy for each other.'

The young man smiled sadly.

'You know what? I'm not crazy, I'm just baffled. The more I hate her, the more I love her. We were good together once, and then we weren't good together any more. At least I wasn't good with her any more.'

Adam took no notice of him and began to study the card. The blood from Atakan's hand had covered half the image on the front of the card, but the other half was clear enough. The image was of an Egyptian pyramid, beneath which was printed *PYRAMID*. On the back of the card there was a name and a number: *Cleopatra, No. 5*. There are two kinds of people with expensive cards like this: fashion designers and expensive prostitutes. And since half the fun of any vampire story is due to darling whores satisfying a sexual need, Adam knew what kind of person the owner of the card would be. He looked at his companion.

'Good work, son. Let's search the rest of the house and then we can go for supper. You need a proper shower before that, and we both need a change of clothes. We can't go to a brothel looking like this.'

'Do you think one day we will be able to wear posh, expensive clothes to look like upper-class people?'

'No, son,' Adam answered sadly. 'In order to be a true upper-class citizen, a man needs a loving wife and well-behaved children. You and I have been forgotten by women, nature and God. We will never experience happiness. Why? In my case I know that I do not deserve it. In your case, well, ask God why you don't deserve it.'

They stayed in the house until late afternoon. They found an empty basement, which in Adam's mind metamorphosed into a chamber that Sarah at some point may have used to torture vampires. *Once the heart and mind is broken, it can no longer imagine beauty; it simply creates decay and hopelessness.*

*

After a long shower, Atakan stood looking at the steamy mirror. He wiped part of the mirror with his hand and watched how the steam transformed into warm droplets of water. He put the same hand on his head and started tapping it.

Meanwhile, Adam was sitting on the two-seater sofa in the living room. He started to wonder whether Sarah had had a lover after her divorce. The old, tired hunter closed his eyes and remembered her as a young woman; he did not remember her face, but her long blonde hair dancing in the wind. Her face used to make him happy, but he hadn't been able to remember either the face or that happiness for such a long time. He remembered when she had pointed her finger towards the shining sun; that day Adam was happy, that day he dreamt of having a family, that day he was ready to change … that day was gone and dead forever. Now he was alone in his world with pain and his collection of vampire fangs from previous hunts. Now, in his mind, he was what he had been born to be: one big nothing.

They decided on an outdoor restaurant in one of the small villages outside the city. The broken wooden benches populated the space, and they went and sat down. Atakan ordered a bottle of wine for himself and some chicken soup; Adam went with the rare-cooked steak. At a table next to them was a young girl, sitting alone. She had a red Kurdish headband around her short, curly black hair and was busy with her drawings; an art student taking solace in the countryside to enhance her vision on beauty.

The two men did not talk until their food arrived.

Then Atakan asked, 'Why are you so interested in Sarah's … how shall I put it? Her sudden journey.'

Adam sliced through the steak with his carving knife; the blood oozed out of the meat. He touched it with his index finger and then sucked the blood off his skin. He then told Atakan about his encounter with Christopher.

Atakan began to chuckle and said in a low voice, 'As far as I know, we may be on a wild goose chase.'

Adam continued eating. 'We found a card, didn't we? Besides, we need to follow up on things until we are sure they mean nothing.'

Atakan pointed to his teeth. 'And then you will collect more.'

Adam ignored his comment and stared at the way Atakan was eating the soup. He could see the small pieces of mushroom entering his mouth; he could hear the sound of those mushrooms being chewed. He put his knife and fork down.

'Why do you keep calling your mother by her first name?' he asked. 'She was good to you, wasn't she?'

Atakan shrugged his shoulders and said nothing.

Adam continued. 'What's your problem with her, huh? You wanted to come and work for us, remember? She put in a nice word for you, didn't she? She always spoke highly of you. The very last time I saw her, she was still saying what a loving, caring son you were, even though I know you hadn't spoken to her in months. I bet you didn't even send her a card for Christmas or her birthday.'

'You have problems with your own mother, everybody knows it. Why are you picking on me?'

Adam became angry. 'No, you are wrong. I don't hate my mother. I just want to suffocate her, since she's such a two-faced back-stabbing bitch. My mother has the same feelings for me as I have for her, but at least we send each other boxes of chocolate … although they have a small amount of poison inside them. Besides, we are talking about your issues, not mine.'

'Really, though, why do you hate her so much?' Atakan persisted.

'None of your damn business.'

Atakan rubbed his bald head.

'Well, I just hate people, and Sarah happened to be there. That's all.'

'She happened to be there? Really, boy?'

Atakan drank some of his wine.

'I guess I'm just like you, I have no conscience.' Then he added sarcastically, 'Brother, at least we are pure of such high morality.'

At this point the young girl with the Kurdish headband came over to their table and said, 'Excuse me? Can I take your time for a second?'

And without waiting for them to answer, she sat at their table.

In a passionate, kind, nurturing voice, she said to Adam, 'You know, in Barcelona artists like me sometimes draw half the face of a man or woman and then show it to them. If they like their portrait, the artist finishes the work and gets paid for it. Now, I have done the same for you.'

She put the drawing of Adam on the table. It was, indeed, half of his face. It looked old, tired, lost. Adam put 20 pounds on the table for the girl and then turned the drawing round.

The girl picked up the money and said in a friendly manner, 'But I didn't finish it. Let me finish the portrait first.'

Adam looked at her kindly.

'Fuck off, love!' he said calmly.

The girl left the table, shocked and insulted.

'As I was saying, we are free from morality,' Atakan said softly.

'Shut up! Let's go to my house and change our clothes. Remember, we need to visit a brothel. This job never fails to disappoint.'

*

Adam called the number on the card and heard the strong, business-like voice of an old lady on the other end.

'Hello, ma'am,' he said confidently. 'A friend of mine has introduced your good establishment to me, and I was wondering if I might pay my respects by coming to the Pyramid. I will be accompanied by a friend.'

The lady answered kindly, 'Of course, sir. I would like to say that I welcome you to our club, which is more like an honourable family. The entrance fee to our house is 1,000 pounds per person, and our shows are free. However, whatever happens after the shows is between our guests and our family members. If the individual who accompanies you is a lady, we have a certain area that includes our lesbian family members. Of course, you can go to this area as well; for you in this area, only looking and talking are allowed. No touching; no physical tenderness.'

'Excellent, ma'am. My companion is a gentleman. May I have the address, please?'

As he wrote down the address, he thanked the lady and put the phone down. He looked at Atakan.

'Well, thank God for FATHER's credit card. You know what? I believe we are in the wrong business. I should have gone into the sex industry; I would have been quite wealthy by now.'

Atakan looked indifferent.

'I need to use the toilet,' he said, and went upstairs.

Adam's house looked the same as the last time he had been there: well organised and clean, but soulless. It was obvious that it lacked the warmth of a family. That's the thing about family; its warm breath helps a man let go of all his pain for a few seconds, but this house had never experienced those few seconds … Adam did not experience those few seconds.

Atakan heard a banging noise coming from downstairs and thought it must be the old man trying to make some tea. The young hunter mistakenly entered Adam's bedroom instead of the bathroom, and saw that everything was in order except the cross hanging upside down on the far wall. A faint smile appeared on his face; he looked carefully behind him to make sure that he had not been followed. Then he took a small camera out of his jacket and took a picture of the cross.

'Poor old man. He is really fighting with God.'

He proceeded to the left corner of the bedroom; he was interested in a small room, only a little bigger than a closet, attached to the main bedroom. He remembered that many years ago, when he was just a boy, he had been inside that small room and felt very scared. He opened the small door and went inside; the horror and shock he had felt came back to him. He looked at the shelves, on which sat small bottles containing alcohol and vampire fangs; the alcohol would maintain the fangs' integrity. There were hundreds of fangs: the anthropology museum of the sadness of a lonely hunter, that's what it was. He took a photo of the collection and then went back to the bathroom.

He did not like what he saw there either. A couple of used blades were in the sink, on which were dried bloodstains. He took photos of those too.

After he had done his business, he flushed, returned to the bedroom and lay down on Adam's bed. There was something he had never understood: the old man did not speak about women. He couldn't flirt with them, yet he had slept with many. Atakan was amazed how those women would agree to be with the old hunter, and yet Adam never let any of them into his life. It was like he had already found the perfect woman and lost her to the same power that had taken everything from him: destiny. He had gone from one woman to another, trying to compensate for losing that perfection. But the more he spent time with them, the bigger the empty space of that perfection became. He finally gave up and preferred to punish himself. The loneliness had begun.

The young hunter rolled over on the bed and touched the pillow on the other side; he knew if his mother had ever slept with Adam, he would not be able to convince himself to be in this bed. He would hate his mother even more. He remembered it was her who had asked Adam if she could show his fang collection to her son. This had been Atakan's eighth birthday gift; ironically, all he had asked for was a MacDonald's.

CHAPTER 5

"Salomé, Salomé, dance for me. I pray thee dance for me. I am sad to-night. Yes, I am passing sad to-night. When I came hither I slipped in blood, which is an evil omen; and I heard, I am sure I heard in the air a beating of wings, a beating of giant wings. I cannot tell what they mean ... I am sad to-night. Therefore dance for me. Dance for me, Salomé, I beseech you. If you dance for me you may ask of me what you will, and I will give it you, even unto the half of my kingdom."

Oscar Wilde

Manipulation is one of the best ways to deal with decent people in modern society; of course, the word decent is misused these days. On the other hand, honesty is the only way to deal with society's indecent people; of course, the word indecent is also misused these days. Prostitutes are surely easy targets to be criticised; many ladies and gentlemen of society would tell you that they cannot believe how someone could want to sell his or her body. No matter how accepting people are of them nowadays, there is a part of the human psyche that still has derogatory views of their behaviour. We should also not forget our two-faced friends, the so-called decent people who work in banks, hospitals, schools, universities and other places. They enjoy the services of prostitutes more than the so-called indecent people, such as writers, actors and aristocrats. Nothing had destroyed human civilisation during history like the acts of decent middle-class people.

In a brothel you can find the pillar of society who is always busy working for charities; they smile at you, they may even buy you a drink. Many long-term friendships among charitable people have been formed in a brothel. Doctors, lecturers, scientists and priests are the main customers. Of course, there would be no Muslim imam there; they are probably so busy with running the day-to-day business of that blissful place that the poor men have no time to take a bite out of one of their employees. Oh, the tragic life of working people. The funny thing about all of this is that these imams run so many brothels for the sake of God's glory, or at least this is their explanation for why they do what they do.

Adam Helsing was far too damaged an individual to be concerned with the *politique de bordel*. He wanted to focus on finding Cleopatra No. 5. He let the events of the next few minutes be fast-forwarded in his mind, in the way a depressing French film narrative would progress: shave and shower – cut – put on a clean and nice suit – cut – go to the garage and get the vampire killer kit ready – cut – back to house – cut – I am wearing the wrong shirt, it is white, so if I pull the fangs out and remove the head, blood will be everywhere. Hmm, blood, it reminds me of the jam Aunt Judie made and sent to me in the summer of 1958, or was it 1959? Hey, where was I? Oh yes, my shirt; I will go with the black one – cut – inside the car, smell of burnt burger; damn, I wish it smelt of burnt vampire testicles, since it is the same scent as the decaying body of one's grandmother. Oh well, one can't be picky – cut – the front door; I have forgotten to close it. Further brain activity: I am ready to hunt again. In the car, ready to kill and torture – cut – damn, the engine won't start. We need to hire a posh car; never arrive at a brothel in a taxi. They'll know you're poor and treat you like your girlfriend, dishonestly.

Adam and Atakan hired a Mercedes Benz. It was not the newest of models, but it was clean and presentable. It didn't have that burnt burger scent either.

As they drove away, Adam asked, 'Have you ever been inside one of these brothels to find vampires?'

'I have killed vampires who were visiting the girls, but no, I've never killed a vampire in a brothel; I've never known a vampire who worked as a prostitute.'

Driving a little faster, Adam said, 'You know, sometimes we spoke about this with your mother. We were ... well, now that she is gone, I am *still* jealous of vampires.'

Atakan looked at him with confusion in his eyes. 'What do you mean?'

'I mean, look at them. They are always well dressed. They talk politely. They are most likely rich. It's like there is a force inside them that makes them stronger and makes them despise the hardships of life. I am jealous of their pride. You know, it's like that poem by D. H. Lawrence about self-pity. You know the one?'

'Oh yes, professor! Literature was my favourite topic at school,' he said sarcastically.

Adam ignored him and went on.

'Lawrence wrote: *I never saw a wild thing sorry for itself.* You know, Atakan, it's the story of those vampires. I saw them dying and it wasn't beautiful or poetic. But somehow, as they went down, their pride and dignity lived on. Even after they perished, I could feel their strength around me. That, my boy, used to be the sign of a great person dying in the old days. In my lifetime I have never seen a human who died with that pride in their eyes.'

Atakan was silent for a while.

'Do you like them?' he asked eventually.

'I hate myself; how can I like anybody else? I envy them. I envy how peaceful they are with themselves. That will never happen to me.'

'I saw the blades in your bathroom, they had dried blood on them, and it was fresh. Can't you just forget about what's happened and move on? More importantly, can't you get over yourself and move on?'

Adam gave a sad smile. 'You sound like your mother, my dad, Christopher and everyone else. No, I can't move on. I am like an embryo nurtured in a womb of pain and trauma; it grows and grows, but it is never born.'

'What do you think will happen to this embryo in the end?'

Adam sighed. 'Well, I think when Alice failed to leave the wonderland, a roaring fire freed her from the enchanted dream.'

They did not talk for the rest of their trip; the car's radio was on the news. Parliament had reduced social benefits for single mothers, which could mean some of those mothers would join brothels. Meanwhile, the PM's wife was complaining that Number 10 was not warm enough, and Parliament had agreed to modernise the new heating system.

The Pyramid was in fact a seventeen-century mansion, with gates made of solid bronze on which was carved a large letter P. The massive gardens were full of oak trees and red roses, which had been looked after perfectly. The hedges were trimmed to look like an army of sphinxes, and there were Egyptian-style vases on both sides of the driveway that were in fact giant-sized gas lights, illuminating the road to the show of intimacy.

The house's luxurious facade suggested to the illustrious visitors that they were not at a shabby dirty brothel like those in Amsterdam or London. This was a house of class, similar to those in Prague, Vienna and Warsaw.

As they reached the main entrance, a handsome young African man was waiting for them. He was wearing light-brown baggy pants and a plain red waistcoat on which was an image of Qetesh, the Egyptian goddess of fertility. The young man's right nipple was pierced with a big black pearl, and he was wearing two golden earrings.

As the vampire hunters stepped out of the car, the young man approached them. Adam handed him the car key.

They entered the building and a rather large man appeared in front of them, wearing the same outfit as the young janitor.

'Good evening, gentlemen,' he said in a deep voice, 'and welcome to the Pyramid. I gather this is your first visit? I have not seen your proud, charming faces before in our fine palace of pleasure. Please correct me if I am wrong.'

Adam smiled. 'We are new.'

'Indeed; not new to the art of erotic pleasures, but humble strangers to this ancient house of ours. As old as heaven, as powerful as the gods and as welcoming as one's beloved's beauty. Madam Goodwill will be here shortly to show you around. It is customary in the Pyramid for new visitors to be greeted by the queen of the house.'

Following this elegant introduction to the estate, the man disappeared.

As soon as he was gone, Atakan said, 'Jesus, Joseph and Mary; these pimps have more class and manners than lawyers.'

'God bless this job of ours.'

Suddenly, the madam appeared. She was very well dressed, in a black coat and a long black skirt, and wearing very light make-up. She was in her late fifties, with long red hair. If you had seen her on a coach or the Tube, you would think she was a bank manager or a successful businesswoman, not a brothel *mama*.

She smiled at the two fish out of water.

'Good evening, gentlemen. I am Madam Goodwill. I hope you had a pleasant journey to our Pyramid. Now, if you will permit me, there are a few formalities that we need to go through. First things first; may I obtain the entrance fees?'

'Yes, ma'am … I mean madam,' Adam said, and handed her his credit card.

She took it and smiled professionally.

'I will see to this shortly. Now, the Pyramid is all about life, and in life we must choose. On your right you have the gentlemen's section. On your left you have the ladies' section. Of course, men will be men. You can go to the ladies' section, but as I said on the phone, no touching. What is your choice?'

'Can we see both, please? Atakan exclaimed.

The madam laughed like a Victorian lady, while Adam looked at his young companion with disbelief.

'What my young friend means is, since we are here, it would be a shame to miss the opportunity to see the entire wealth of your fine establishment.'

'I entirely agree with you,' she said approvingly.

She then asked them to follow her. As they discovered the inside of the building, their faces froze with admiration.

The gentlemen's section had four areas. The first was the main hall, where paintings of Egyptian gods and goddesses covered the walls and ceiling. There was no electricity here, and instead the space was filled with huge red lanterns containing candles. Size certainly mattered in the Pyramid. Adam walked round in a circle and was overwhelmed by the beauty of the place.

The second area was where the party rooms were located. These rooms were not for people to play video games with the prostitutes; for that kind of brothel, you'd need to travel to Tokyo.

The third area was on the second level above the main hall. It was covered with purple curtains, behind which loud laughter and music could be heard.

The fourth area was the drinking area, and was for the more sublime visitors.

Adam saw an old, well-dressed man entering this area, and realised that he knew him. He was a famous TV comedian who used to run shows gathering money for under-privileged children. *How many children could his entry fee to Pyramid save?* Adam wondered.

'Well, if you want to see our ladies, you can go to the show room,' Madam Goodwill told them, and left with the credit card.

Adam said to his young companion, 'Remember, we are here for one thing and one thing only, work. Let's go and meet Cleopatra No. 5.'

They entered the show room, which was located behind a curtain on which was the image of a small ark. It reminded Adam of the question Sarah had asked in her notes.

Behind the curtain was the biggest venue Adam had seen in his life. There were at least forty men and around twenty-five girls, all of whom wore ancient Egyptian dresses and pure gold bracelets on which was the image of Qetesh.

The old hunter said, 'These girls make more in a single night than your mother made in two months. Life is a well-written dark comedy.'

There was a group of five older prostitutes in the middle of the show room dancing to some very strange music that Adam had never heard before, a combination of African classic drum beats and Hungarian folklore singing. It was neither happy nor sad, but very addictive. A feeling of numbness suddenly took over him.

'This music makes you high,' he said.

'No, old man, it is not the music. It is the powder.'

Atakan pointed to three big horn-shaped objects at the three corners of the room, which formed a triangle. Some sort of powder was coming from these horns and morphing into a black cloud. The cloud was a mushroom of ecstasy above the girls, men and dancers. This cloud was pure euphoria.

'You are not made for this room,' Atakan continued. 'I'll find your No. 5 and bring her to you.'

Adam agreed, and left the room.

As Atakan stood there, he felt that he too was succumbing to the false happiness of the cloud. Suddenly, the bony fingers of the Maestro touched him on the shoulder. He turned round and stared at the two empty holes in the musician's skull.

The rotten teeth parted and the man said, 'Son, you always have the cemetery powder. Please don't fall into taking whatever medicine they serve here.'

Atakan slapped his own face and went looking for the girl he had come to find.

*

Once outside the show room, Adam felt much more at ease, and could breathe the clean air into his lungs. He told himself that he was too old for a place like this. He knew men older than him who would disagree, but they had a good excuse: they were all married and had children.

He went to the drinking area, which was populated with short tables and even shorter chairs. In the centre of every table was a statue of Ra, God of Sun, in the shape of a hawk holding a burning candle in its claws.

Adam sat down on one the chairs; his knees were almost into his belly. 'Wrong,' said a voice.

Adam looked round, and in the corner of the almost dark room he saw a shining red dot. The dot began to move and came closer. It was the Painter's ruby ring, but it was not on his finger; he was holding it in his hand.

He looked at Adam and said, 'Sit properly, Japanese style, and your knees will fit perfectly beneath the table.'

Adam did as he was advised, and his knees fitted perfectly. The Painter joined him and sat on the other side of the table. Adam looked directly into his companion's eyes and wondered if those ancient and somehow wise eyes justified the stare.

'You look familiar,' he said.

The Painter placed the ring back on his finger.

'Not the first thing to say to someone inside a brothel. Usually, people would ask how much.'

Adam laughed for a moment. 'Well, you don't look like a whore. Maybe you were one in a previous life.'

'I have always been who I am, and I'm not from here. That being said, I am the vision behind this establishment. It took me ten years to design and build it. I don't own it, but I still enjoy coming here. Why are you here? No disrespect, but you are not the type of person to usually attend a place of such class. Your jacket is not tailored; you are made for, let me tease you, a third-class teahouse located in the Midlands.'

'Good one, Mr Vision. The drinks are on me; what should I order for you?'

Both men settled on red Merlot, a vintage of 2000. In a short time a small vase arrived with two blue suns painted on either side of its handles, together with two small crystal glasses that were placed in front of them. Adam poured some wine for himself and his companion.

'What should we drink to?' the Painter asked.

Adam thought for a moment. 'In memory of the time that we used to say, I will never go inside a brothel for any reason.'

'Good days; good old dead days.'

Both men emptied their glasses.

At that moment, Madam Goodwill arrived and walked straight over to Adam.

She held his credit card in front of him and said, 'Your card has been declined, sir.'

Adam felt as if a small ice cube had been pushed into his underpants. He was about to say something when his drinking companion came to his rescue.

'It is all right. Put it on my account. Dr Helsing is an old friend.' Then he took charge of pouring some more wine into their glasses.

As soon as the madam had left their table, Adam asked in amazement, 'How do you know my name?'

The Painter sipped his wine.

'I attended a conference a long time ago where you were one of the speakers. You were young, passionate, a real visionary. You appeared to be happy and full of hope, two things that always work well together. You gave a speech on the concept of ugliness and its position in the human psyche. I still remember your words. You said…'

The Painter jumped up suddenly, straightened his body and spoke loudly, as if talking to an imaginary audience.

'…ladies and gentlemen.'

The other people drinking in the room turned round and looked at him, but he continued.

'Ugliness is not the opposite of beauty, nor is it an evil concept. It has been, and always will be, an independent living organ of human mentality. Being ugly does not mean a man or a woman is not beautiful.'

At this moment the Painter held his hands in the shape of a cross and walked to the middle of the room.

'We think our enemies are ugly,' he shouted passionately, 'not because they are ugly in their features, but because we are intimidated by them; we want to create a fault in their existence so that we can gather our courage to fight them. This is what I have to say: our enemies have been dealing with the same kind of fear that we are now dealing with. They too think the opposite party, us, is ugly. We are both wrong; there is only one path to victory: to ignore what beauty and ugliness are, and then do what you want to do. Those who want to kiss the lips of victory shall walk through the shadow of death.'

He finished his speech and returned to his seat. Others in the room had returned to their drinking without paying any more attention to the Painter. Adam clapped his hands.

'What about other people's rights? That was the question that someone in the audience asked, but I can't remember the answer I gave.'

The Painter finished his drink.

'I remember; you said, think of the next man as your competitor for the last ticket of the last available ferry before clergymen attack the city. Some members of the audience laughed, some didn't say anything, and a couple of priests complained. And I, well, I was simply mesmerised by you.'

Adam poured the last of the wine into his glass.

'If I had known that I had such a huge fan, I would have continued to be an academic. Things changed without me having any control over them. At least that's what I keep telling myself. I have been living unhappily for a long time.'

Adam was about to ask his new friend's name, but Atakan entered the room. Even from a distance Adam could smell the smoke and drugs coming from his clothes; however, the young hunter was sober.

He came over to Adam and whispered in his ear, 'I'm sorry to interrupt, but there is someone who wants to meet us in one of the rooms.'

'Great.' The old hunter looked at the Painter and said, 'I'm sorry, but I need to leave.'

'To see any of the girls, you need to pay. That is also on my account, Doctor. By the way, beauty suggests far more ugliness than ugliness itself.'

*

Atakan and Adam entered one of the rooms in the corridor. It was spacious and in the shape of a triangle. There was a circular bed in the centre, which was covered by the skin of adult Cambodian cobras. There were three lanterns, one at each corner of the room. On the edge of the bed sat a tall, slender young girl with long black hair and striking green eyes. Each knuckle on her hands was pierced with a tiny gold coin.

Adam looked at her lustfully, and forgot all about his ideal talks on beauty and ugliness. *This woman, this girl, it doesn't matter if she is human or vampire, she is Venus herself,* he thought. Adam looked around the room and saw a big sofa over which was draped the white skin of a sheep. He sat down on the sofa, and Atakan joined him.

'Are you lovers?' asked the girl.

Atakan said to Adam, 'I think it's for the best if you stand up and I sit alone on the sofa.'

'No, I think it is better if you stand up and I sit,' the old hunter suggested.

'I have been standing in the show room while you were sitting. I'm tired.'

'I have been living and standing for two or three decades longer than you. I'm more tired.'

'Fine, we'll both sit. I'm not homophobic … and I'm sure that I'm straight.'

'So am I.'

They both remained seated on the sofa.

'If you two bitches are done fighting over the last pair of shoes in the sales,' the girl said, 'I'd like to hear what you want to know. Have you been sent by Sarah?'

'So you knew Sarah Murphy?' Adam asked.

'Why the past tense?'

'It was all over the news; she has been murdered.'

A shiver ran through Cleopatra's calm exterior. Suddenly, she started to talk rapidly and a little hysterically.

'I don't watch TV, I don't read anything other than the texts I receive on my mobile, and I don't like the Internet; it's full of perverts.'

Adam smiled. 'I know she told you about her job. I work for the same company and want to finish her assignment. Tell me what you told her.'

'And the magic word is?' she said mockingly.

Atakan was becoming frustrated.

'Listen to me, you little–'

Adam put his hand on Atakan's shoulder to stop him saying any more.

The old hunter stood up and went over to the bed. He sat down next to the young prostitute, took her hands in his and said, 'Sweetheart, you aren't a maiden and I'm not a saint. You and I first indulged in the forbidden fruit a very long time ago. Now, please, if you don't mind, tell me all you know.'

'Well, I have different clients; different shapes, different sexes, different ages. Of course, they all want the same thing from me, and, well, I always

want the same thing from them. In this job you tend to forget the faces of
your clients; that's easy. You don't fall in love, for love always hurts. When
you love someone, they will morph into a beautiful butterfly. You either
let that butterfly fly away so that she is taken from you, or you hold onto
her long enough until she is crushed in your hands. That is why love never
works; sex does not come from love, but from an arrangement. Some are
clever enough to make money out of it. I have forgotten all my clients except
one. He was tall, handsome and, well, very rich. I met him a few times here
and then he asked me out. I told myself, why not? And then guess what?'

Adam gave a sigh. 'Love is the deadliest of assassins.'

'Exactly,' said the girl.

She removed the scarf from around her neck to reveal two classic
vampire bite marks.

'What happened to the man?' Adam asked.

'Well, as I changed, I became stronger. I resented him for what he had
done to me, but I would hate to be a vampire. One night, I went to his
house and killed him. But then the strangest thing happened. I found a
diary in his house. I'm not ashamed to say that after killing him, I searched
for money or jewellery or some valuable objects, but all I found was that
damn diary.'

'What was in it?'

'There were details of an organisation; a family, it was called. There were
names and other stuff, like 'a sapphire and an emerald'. Then there was a
map that showed where the red object was. The journal read: the sapphire
is in the chest; where is the other gem?'

'And then did you meet Sarah?'

'Yes, I did. She first saw me one night near Croydon, when I was hunting
for fresh blood. It was like she could smell who I was. She overpowered me
and was about to kill me, but I begged her like I had never begged anyone
in my life before. She wouldn't listen, but then I told her about the diary. I
knew she was a probably a hunter. My maker has warned me about them.
She loved the diary and let go of me.'

'And then she came back to you?' suggested Adam.

'She wanted me to get in touch with a few people whose names were in the diary. She mentioned your name to me, Adam Helsing; the only man that a woman can trust. That is why, when your bald friend told me you wanted to see me, I did not escape. Sarah told me that if I helped her, she would give me a medicine that would change me back to my human form. I gathered the information she wanted and then got in touch with her to tell her what I had found. The thing is, none of those people in the diary got back to me. Since I turned into a vampire, I have lived inside a coffin in the basement of my maker's house. One night when I got back, there was a letter that had been delivered to the house; it was for my maker. I opened it, and it read: *25th; Louver; Becky.*'

Adam ran his right hand through his short hair.

'Interesting. Did you tell Sarah?'

'I wanted to,' said the girl, 'but she didn't show up. When I reached the coffee shop where we were supposed to meet, it was in flames. I couldn't see her anywhere. There has been no news about her until today, when your friend here told me that Adam Helsing wanted to talk to me.'

Atakan shuffled on the sofa.

'Well, Sarah is dead. Did you tell anybody else about all this?'

'I swear, I told no one. I am trapped in this body, but I want to change. I want to go back to being a human. Was she right, Doctor? Can you help me? Can I trust you? She told me you know how I can be free from this curse.'

'Yes, you can,' said the old vampire hunter.

He swiftly took a small gun out of his pocket and shot a bullet at her chest. A small hole appeared in her cleavage. As she touched the hole, a blue light appeared around the wound. Then thick blue liquid began to ooze out, and she fell to the floor. As her mouth opened to grasp some air, Adam and Atakan could see her fangs, white, long and sharp. She was in pain, but didn't scream.

Adam went and sat on the floor next to her. He took a pair of pliers out of his jacket pocket and removed her fangs. Blue blood was now pouring out of her mouth. Her pained eyes looked desperately at Adam.

He touched the dying girl tenderly, like a psychopathic lover, and said in a paternal voice, 'I used to trust people; then I realised that if I wanted to live, I needed to stop trusting them.'

A few seconds later, Cleopatra's body dissolved into ashes; they weren't grey, but a blue colour, and shone like crystals.

Adam looked at Atakan.

'Get rid of the ashes,' he ordered. 'We must leave.'

CHAPTER 6

There is a certain relief in change, even though it be from bad to worse! As I have often found in travelling in a stagecoach, that it is often a comfort to shift one's position, and be bruised in a new place.

Washington Irving

Atakan took a finger-size glass vial out of his pocket that contained an amber-coloured liquid. The young hunter bent down and poured the liquid over the ashes. Adam was watching this procedure intently. As soon as he turned around and headed towards the door, Atakan picked up some of the ashes and put them in his pocket. The rest were dissolved in the amber liquid. Soon, all that was left of the vampire was her jewellery, and the ex-hero of the working class put that in his pocket too.

As the two men left the room, the Pyramid was getting busier. Adam looked around.

'I know where Louver is,' he said. 'It is a famous jazz club, sort of an independent venue for younger audiences. We should go.' As they approached the main corridor, Adam said in a low voice, 'We need lots of weapons. I have this gut feeling there may be more than one or two vampires.'

A brunette girl passed them, and Adam followed her with concerned eyes. She took no notice of him and went directly to the area that was for the female customers.

'Are you okay?' Atakan asked him.

In a rather troubled voice, Adam replied, 'You take the car and wait for me outside the main gate. I need a few minutes here.'

'There is no time for the toilet.'

'Do as I tell you,' Adam said in a loud voice.

He left Atakan on his own and followed the brunette. He opened the door and entered the lesbian section of the brothel, an area that was quite similar to the other except that there was a small corridor with a board hanging overhead, on which was written: *For those who cannot touch*. He remembered what the madam had told him. He looked down the corridor and saw that there were ten booths, five located on each side. Adam peeped inside one of them. It had two sections, separated by a glass window. There was one armchair on each side of the window and a wooden hawk-shaped device, clearly for communication.

Adam exited the booth and saw a short girl walking down the corridor.

'I'm looking for a brunette girl. She just came down here,' he said.

The short girl looked at him and began to scratch her nose.

'Well, there are many brunettes around here. But Marian is brunette and she just arrived. Wanna talk to her?'

'Yes,' Adam replied.

'Well, you need to go inside one of the booths and call her name. If she is free, she will come and talk to you. There is a small shelf under the glass; you need to put 50 pounds in there for 5 minutes and push it forward.'

'Okay. What will happen then?'

'She will talk to you. You'll be able to see her, but she won't be able to see you; you will be invisible to her.'

Adam followed her instructions, and a few seconds later he called the name Marian and the girl he was searching for appeared. She was wearing a yellow silk bikini covered in blue snakes.

She sat behind the window and said to the ghost on the other side, 'Hi, baby.'

'It's your dad, Leto,' said Adam.

Leto answered, 'Uh, well, I can't see you because of the glass. Anyway, this glass has been between us for years.'

'Aren't you surprised to hear my voice in here?' asked the self-abusive father.

'No, you were an animal, like any other person I know. What do you want, Adam?'

'I thought you were at university,' said the hapless father.

'Adam, Adam, Adam, how pathetic you are. I am finished with that nonsense; I got my PhD. Like father, like daughter. We both sleep with ladies, don't we? I just get paid for it.'

'No, no!' he screamed. 'Not my own daughter. I … I–'

Leto interrupted him. 'Come on, Adam! You are too weak to say the forbidden word, love. You are incapable of saying it.'

He had tears in his eyes. 'You're the only person I'm concerned about. I send you emails, letters, but you always ignore me. I have tried to reach you, but you were unresponsive. Ignore me if you like, but don't ignore yourself. You're too good to be here.'

'Oh no, I'm not. You see, I want to adopt this young boy, but they wouldn't let me because I didn't have a full-time job. And now I have a full-time job still they don't give me my son, because my job is not good enough for the law. You know what? Fuck them. I will save enough money and kidnap him.'

'Please don't talk like this,' Adam said in despair.

'You know, Adam, I hate men … thanks to you. I want to create the perfect man out of my own son, so other men, men like you, can learn how to be a real man. Our time is up.'

Adam put the money on the shelf and pushed it towards Leto. She took the money, smelt it and waved it in front of the glass, then put it in her bikini bottoms. She gave her father a nasty smile. Her eyes looked like two oceans of hatred ready to release their wrath upon him.

Adam put his hand on the glass.

'Let me help you. I'm unhappy, but I can't change that. I know I wasn't nice to your mother. The thing is, whenever I tried to be a caring husband, this hand, this invisible hand, always prevented me. I just can't do it; in every woman I meet I see my own failure as a man. The image of *the perfect woman* is like a chain around my neck; I can't break free. I want you, Leto; you're my only chance of happiness. It sounds selfish, but I want you. I'm tired; every day I wake up and hate Adam Helsing more than the day before.'

She gave him a very sad, humane smile. 'Well, there is one thing you can do.'

'I will do anything to bring us back together.'

'You can die, or even better, you can kill yourself to be free from all this unhappiness.'

She bent over, kissed the glass and left.

Adam sat there for a minute and cried silently. Then he wiped his eyes, put on a fake strong face and left the booth.

As the rented car took the two hunters away from the Pyramid, Adam said to Atakan in a confident voice, 'Find a pharmacy. I need to buy some steel blades.'

*

By midnight they had already returned to Adam's house and they went straight to the basement. The old man removed the tiles from the floor and took out two big gym bags, each containing different weapons including knives, hammers, short swords, pistols, machine guns and small purple ball-size bombs on which was the image of a wolf's head. Atakan looked at this collection.

'Thank God you're retired,' he said. 'If you weren't, what would you keep here?'

Adam shrugged his shoulders. 'I'm not retired; I'm just not killing vampires any more. Tomorrow night, tomorrow night...' He paused to reflect.

Each of the hunters picked up one of the bags and they ascended to the living room. As they put the fighting gear down, Adam began to wonder how he would feel if instead of all these weapons, he was surrounded by children and grandchildren. No matter how depressed he felt, he could still imagine living with a loving, caring family.

The old hunter left Atakan alone and went into the kitchen, and soon came back with a bottle of white wine and two tall glasses. He sat on the sofa and poured them both a drink.

Adam asked his young companion, 'Do you ever want to have a family and be happy?'

Atakan leaned back against the wall and slowly slid down until he was sat on the floor. He put his index finger inside his glass and began to stir the wine.

'Well … I mean, I'm so … well, you know what we are. We can't really be happy. If it were meant to happen, it would have done a long time ago. There's no point in getting involved with someone properly, deeply, seriously. We would just bring them misery. What is happiness anyway? I really don't know any happy couples.'

Adam sighed. 'The question is, how many happy single individuals do you know? I was in East Asia a few years back. It was full of these old people who were going from one doomed relationship to another with young, poor local boys and girls. They looked happy on the outside; they were holding hands, and laughing and kissing. The same show that couples put on back home. But I couldn't ignore the stench of decay that was coming from their lungs.'

Atakan laughed. 'Well, maybe their lungs were sick or something.'

Adam smiled briefly and continued. 'It was no illness of the flesh. It was the rotten smell of youth's false promises. It was the ashes of the burnt corpses of our dreams.'

He stood up, still holding the glass in his hand.

'I was somebody once,' he continued. 'I had students; they looked up to me, and I looked up to them. Then there was a tragedy; people did not understand what I was crying for. We talked, but nothing really helped. Of course, when people don't want to help you, they will say it was you who did not want to get better. So I did the only practical thing I could do, and poured oil on my soul and burned it all. To hell with my research and the students when all hope was dead. I stopped thinking about myself. Once you're in that mansion, you have two choices: either to leave through the front door and do good deeds and then die sad and unhappy, but with dignity; or to leave through the back door and enter the wilderness, where you will hunt to destroy and kill, to compensate for your unhappiness. My father would have left through the front door. I, however, broke free from all morality, goodness and sanity, and left through the back door. No matter what choices you make, every single moment of your life until you die is a mixture of pain and trauma. You fake smiles, you go to parties, yet you keep saying to yourself, if only I were to die, this piercing heart-breaking existence would be over.'

Atakan looked at him with wide, surprised, semi-drunk eyes.

'But you were *somebody* in the Guild and you still are a legend. FATHER trusted you enough to give you a high rank.'

Adam laughed, and then a tear fell from the corner of his left eye.

'My poor, naive friend, in all these years I have achieved nothing. I was a collector of knowledge; I was an agent of love. Now I am a collector of fangs; now I am an agent of death. And I always ask what happens, philosophically, when people die and their death gives birth to vampirism.'

'Who cares? Besides, it's not our concern, is it? If it will help to mend your broken soul, give me a lecture on the subject.'

Adam nodded his head in approval, put down his glass and began.

'Ladies and gentlemen, today's lecture is nothing but a simple story. This has happened to a man I knew. Once upon a time, when people used to travel in carriages, a colonel and his son rode along a deserted country road. It was a frosty December morning, and the good Lord had been generous with snow. As the horses were pulling along the carriage, the son said to his father, "Excuse me, sir, may I ask you a question?" The father shuffled under the big red blanket that was covering them both and said, "You may indeed." The son asked, "Sir, what is eternal life? Does it mean that one never dies?" The father looked at his son and put his hand on the young boy's head. "Young man," he said, "eternal life means that you are not afraid of death. All human concepts will die, but the soul of the courageous man shall live forever and leave its mark on other people's lives." Suddenly, an angry grey wolf appeared in front of them. The driver stopped the carriage and the horses began to rear up in fear. The young boy, who was only 8 years old, jumped down from his warm seat and landed on a huge pile of snow in front of the hungry wolf. As he looked at the beast's menacing, crazy eyes, he absorbed the strength of the wolf and then the boy attacked the predator, jumping on the animal and pulling his jaws apart as far as possible. The beast was in pain, but the boy pulled and pulled until the upper jaw broke and the wolf fell to the ground, dead. The boy threw away the broken jaw as a beautiful maiden throws away the heart of her young lover. The blood from the wolf's mouth covered the ground in a red blanket. The young boy looked at his father; the father looked at his son. No words passed between them, but they both knew that the boy was worthy to carry on his father's legacy.

Atakan looked amazed and asked, 'What is the point of the story?'

'The point is, the young boy was my father and I abandoned him. In exchange, those I loved abandoned me. The point is, I do not deserve my father's name.'

He gave a sad smile of someone whose heart has been broken, and then left the room.

Atakan sat there in silence for a few minutes, thinking about what he had just heard. As he was about to leave the room, he heard a low noise. He looked at the sofa and saw Adam's phone. He picked it up and saw that Christopher was calling. Atakan rejected the call, and when the second call came, he rejected that too, and the third. Finally, a message arrived: *Do not go to Louver tomorrow. Terminate your investigation. Christopher.*

Atakan deleted the phone's history of all incoming calls and messages.

'We do what we do because life hasn't given us any other option,' he whispered.

*

Adam began carving his chest with the blades he had bought, but this time his cries were louder, for he was experiencing not only his own pain, but the suffering of his daughter as well. He was a failure as a son, a husband and a father. Yet he was an expert in areas of which one is supposed to be ignorant.

Atakan heard him sobbing, but ignored it. He took the remaining ashes of the dead vampire out of his pocket and mixed them with some cemetery powder. The combination was far more powerful than any other form of drug. As soon as he sniffed the self-made drug, his vision became vivid and he was able to see voices in 3D, and could hear the seductions and temptations of the aging universe.

At first, he saw the atmosphere around him becoming denser, until the air changed to a pink wave of water. Although he was standing in the middle of the room, he found himself able to surf in this pink sea of melody.

'Oh, this is so cool,' said the Maestro's skeleton as he appeared from behind the wave.

'Hey, where are the little girl and her stepmother?' Atakan shouted.

'They are on the beach, making a sandcastle; they call it *amour*.'

Atakan looked at the beach; the dead musician was right. The little girl and her free-spirited mother were making a huge sandcastle in the shape of a cosy little house; however, half the house was in ruins, while the other half appeared to be cold and dead. They waved at Atakan.

Suddenly, something happened; something that hadn't happened in a long time.

Atakan began to shout, 'Mom? Mom? Where have you been?'

Sarah's voice came back to him. 'I'm here, son.'

As she said this, five skeletons came out of the water and began to sing, *Io morrò ma lieto in core*: *I perish, but I am glad in heart* from Verdi's *Don Carlo*. Sarah was standing amongst of these soprano-skeletons.

Atakan listened to the singing and then spoke again.

'Mom, the war is about to begin, and this time I'm scared.'

'Scared of what, son?'

'Not of death, but of guilt.'

As the song progressed, the son knelt in front of his mother and she put her hands on his head.

'Feel guilty for one thing and one thing only: failing yourself.'

Then she merged into the pink melody and became part of the sea.

As Atakan continued to gaze at the pink sea, the Maestro approached him.

'100 pounds for the opera song that we played for you and your old woman.'

Atakan stared at the greedy skeleton. 'No way! 10.'

'70.'

'40.'

'It's a deal.'

*

The day Atakan and Adam went to the Louver was eventful for people who are concerned with this *monogatari*.

That morning, Christopher woke up alone in his large, expensive empty bed in his large, expensive, cold house, naturally in a bad mood. After the FATHER, he was the wealthiest member of the Guild. He was also one of the few married people who were part of the organisation. That being said, his marriage was an unhappy one. His wife was too good for him; she had made many sacrifices for him in their lives, but in the end, her husband only had devotion and fidelity for the FATHER. The last straw was when she realised that Christopher's money had not come from the family business. A newspaper in Poland had released a report on a Nazi officer who had been a guard at one of the death camps in Poland during the Second World War. The officers had stolen silverware and jewellery from the victims at the camp. The article became a universal story, and the photo of the officer was of Christopher's biological father. After confronting her husband, he admitted his guilt but felt no remorse. It had been three months since their separation.

The first thing the vice-president of the Guild did when he got out of bed was to check his phone. No message had been received from Adam; this was unusual. He wanted to give him a call, but he decided to go and see the old hunter at his home instead.

Christopher hated Adam for many reasons, the most important being that Adam had always managed to find the will to keep fighting. Christopher, on the other hand, was a devoted Catholic and, of course, a charlatan. He was the biggest liar on God's earth, and would manipulate everyone and everything. And he believed he was the only person who knew the extent of FATHER's corruption. Year after year they had managed to manipulate both vampires and humans into making the war drag on and on, for one reason and one reason only: to earn a whole lot of money.

Now, after all these years, thanks to the incompetence of society's political masters, the business of vampire hunting was, sadly, like many other businesses of the middle class, on its knees. FATHER was looking for an intense bloody war with vampires, a war that he could win and use to regain some of his lost reputation, which would grab the attention of new investors in the cause of killing vampires. The problem was, when you don't know where your enemy sleeps, how can you kill him in his bed? Initiating a war was not as simple as FATHER had imagined.

A few months earlier when Christopher received the information about the gems from Sarah, he began his own research, and both he and Adam had come to the same conclusion: Louver. Christopher's men had been inside the Pyramid recording Adam's conversation with Cleopatra No. 5, and tonight was the night for Christopher; the night of the dead.

No one in the Guild except Christopher had knowledge of FATHER's secret killing machine: a group of fifty former Arab terrorists from the Middle East, men who, thanks to FATHER's scientists, had been transformed into zombies. In his heart, Christopher hoped that during the attack on the Louver, Adam would be killed. However, FATHER was aware of Adam's presence in the jazz club and considered him to be very useful for the cause. The only reason Christopher was about to go to Adam's house knowing he was not there, was to give himself an excuse when he was brought in front of FATHER. 'I did all I could,' he would say, 'but he wasn't anywhere to be found. It is a sad occurrence that we have lost a dear old friend.'

Christopher knew that FATHER was not interested in the two gems; they were just a hoax for the Guild president to initiate war. 'If we provide the vampires with a massacre, they will provide us with a war,' he had said.

Christopher stood up straight and heard his joints make their usual early morning clicking noise. He smiled viciously as he imagined Adam dead in the club.

The vice-president went to look at himself in the mirror; he enjoyed observing his own reflection. He touched his moustache and imagined that he was Stalin. He was well aware that the FATHER was an old man and would die sooner or later; then he would replace him. *One narcissist is dead; long live the narcissist.*

As the vice-president got dressed, he began to think about the fifty soldiers; they were savages. *There will be more blood in Louver than in 1789. Adam will die and the war will begin. Once more, the propaganda machine of the Guild will begin to operate and Tartarus will become wealthy for a second time.*

With these thoughts, he ate a hearty breakfast of eggs, mushroom and cold chicken. Then he went outside to the garage and started the car's engine; the radio was on and it was playing Bob Dylan's *Things Have Changed*.

Christopher drove the car slowly out of the garage. Suddenly, out of nowhere a teenage girl appeared in front of his car. She was wearing a traditional Swiss costume and holding a small basket in her left hand. She smiled sweetly at Christopher and he smiled back. *Well, why not? She will be second breakfast. It won't be the first time either*, he thought.

As the girl came near the car, he wound his window down and said charmingly and paternally, 'Hi, dear, are you all right?'

The girl smiled and said in a very strong German accent, 'I think I'm lost.'

'Oh dear. Do you want to come in and play around with my iPod to find where you want to go?'

The girl smiled and brushed her long blonde hair away from her face.

Then, in perfect English, she said, 'I'd prefer to drain your blood for my client.'

'Shite!' was Christopher's answer.

He quickly reached for his gun, but the girl had taken out a handful of yellow crushed grass from her basket and blown them into his face. The grass began to erode the skin tissue and part of his flesh. Christopher couldn't even scream, as his mouth was open when the grass was blown at him and some of it had gone down his throat and burnt his vocal cords. Most of his face was burnt, and blood was dripping onto his shirt.

An ancient-looking van drove past and stopped next to Christopher's car. The teenagers got out of the vehicle, went over to the car, pulled out his half-conscious body and put him inside the van. They were the same people who had killed Sarah Murphy.

Once all the teenagers were inside, the van drove off at speed. The girl in the Swiss clothes took her Galaxy phone out of her pocket and dialled a number.

When the person on the other end answered, she said, 'We've got him,' and then ended the call.

She looked at her companions. 'If things go according to his vision, by this coming Sunday a new phase will have begun.'

One of the boys asked, 'Any word from our employer?'

'Patience and hope.'

*

That day was eventful for Leto as well. By 6 a.m. she was asleep in one of the rooms in the Pyramid. Next to her lay a naked woman in her sixties; a paying customer.

Once again, Leto had her recurrent dream. She was walking in a wintery forest, where the wind threw snow and frost at her face. The bitter cold was too much for her tired, fragile body. She was walking aimlessly inside the jungle; unlike Dante, she had no companion to help her find the road. She was going from nowhere to nowhere.

As she walked on, she saw the shadow of a huge black bat following her. As her goal-less journey progressed, the shadow slowly turned in a different direction. She did not give up, and turned to follow the shadow. The hunted had become the hunter.

It was getting even colder now and she could see thick red clouds bringing a storm. As she picked up her pace, the storm intensified. She managed to hide beneath an old oak tree, where she stayed for hours, days and months, until one day, the storm passed.

She crept out and looked around. There was blood everywhere; the storm had been the prophet of blood. Young Helsing saw a massive bat, perhaps five times bigger than a human, sitting on a branch of the tall oak tree. She studied the anatomy and noticed that it was animal apart from its head, which was the figure of a sad, handsome young man. She moved closer.

'Who are you, gentle friend?' she asked.

The creature laughed sadly and spread his wings wide.

In a deep, kind voice, he said, 'I am a broken man, sister. It is warm under my wings, my heart is shattered, and the blood coming out of it makes my body even warmer.'

She smiled compassionately at the creature and opened her arms.

'Brother, is it not warmer under my wings?'

The bat tilted his head. 'It is always warmer under a woman's wings.' Then he smiled too.

The creature flew down to the ground and wrapped Leto in his arms, and she wrapped him in her own. They gazed into each other's eyes.

'Think of my eyes as a mirror. What do you see?' the bat asked.

Leto gazed back at her reflection in his eyes and said, 'I see beauty gone in darkness. I see dead hope in darkness. I see victory in darkness. I see peace of mind in darkness. I see that kind of freedom in darkness that no angel or man can offer me. In darkness I see myself; I see death.'

The bat embraced her harder.

'Then be free, Leto, daughter of Adam, and teach me to be free too. Be beautiful and teach me to be beautiful. Be victorious and teach me to be victorious. Learn from darkness, and teach me its rules too.' A blue teardrop fell from the corner of his eye.

She looked at the tear and picked it up. She smelt it.

'Awful?' the bat asked.

'No; it is warm and strong.'

He let go of her.

'We all have imperfect bodies; we all are mutated from blood and ugliness,' he said, and then flew away.

Leto looked down at her arms. While holding the bat's body, they had morphed into white wings with light green stripes on them. She flew away to join the bat, and together they mastered the dead, starless night. She observed the fields and forests from the sky and finally saw life: a free-spirited corpse and her young daughter of a skeleton, swimming naked in a lake of blood and fire.

She was about to descend and present herself to mother and child when she was interrupted by a childish voice.

'Hello.'

She turned her head and saw a young boy, no more than 4 or 5 years old, flying next to her and the bat. He had one green eye and one red eye.

Leto looked at him and said, 'Why are your eyes different colours?'

He replied softly, 'The red one is from heaven, and the green one from hell.'

She flew closer to him.

'It won't be easy, you and I being together. They won't let me adopt you.'

The boy flew above her and sat on her shoulders.

'We will be ourselves and we will be together.'

Leto woke up from her dream. She was still in her bed in the Pyramid, lying next to the naked woman. Why had the woman chosen her and not somebody else?

The young prostitute climbed out of the bed and studied her naked body in the mirror. She wanted to adopt a child, and no was not the answer she wanted to hear, but she had heard it all her life. She looked back at her client. The older woman didn't know anything about her, but the latter knew everything about the older woman. She had seen her picture on the news; a rich, successful family lawyer, loved by the nation because they didn't know her.

'We are the people, and we always love things of which we are ignorant,' Leto whispered to herself.

Here she stood, a young woman supposed to be the future of society, the daughter of a man who was also once supposed to be the future of society.

She smiled in sadness and whispered, 'Let's fight; civilisation has taken me to a brothel.'

She went over to the bed and sat next to the sleeping client. She kissed the older woman on the back of her neck.

The lawyer woke up slowly, rolled over and looked at Leto.

'Uhh, what time is it, sweetie?'

'I want to see the life ebb from your eyes.'

And then she swiftly began to strangle the woman. Half awake, half asleep, the client tried to fight back, scratching Leto's face, but the strangulation went on.

When the woman was near death, Leto remembered what her PhD supervisor had once told her: 'Your thesis is not that new. You need novelty in what you want to do.'

Leto loosened her hands. The older woman opened her mouth to scream, but Leto pushed her right hand down on her throat and with two of the fingers on her other hand she pierced the woman's eyes. The symbol of law and decency was blind, naked, dying in a glamorous whorehouse. The nation's favourite hero had never in her life been decent and proper.

It took Leto a few minutes, but finally she had made her first kill; she felt different. In the process of this newfound ability, her face and the wrist of her right had been injured; the trophy of a hunter's first hunt. She got up off the bed.

For the next hour she soaked in a hot bath, and then took all of the money out of the dead lady's bag. As she left the Pyramid, she had a feeling that her arms had never been more ready to hold her child. Death had finally made her a parent.

CHAPTER 7

Only the dead have seen the end of war.

Plato

Christopher could tell that the van was speeding. He could hear Chopin's *Nocturne* playing on the radio. A couple of times, the man whose ego had made him view himself as a demigod lost consciousness. The people who had kidnapped him were in absolute silence; it was like they had some kind of connection with each other that made it unnecessary for them to utter a word.

Then the noise of thunder came, making Christopher regain full consciousness. His hands were tied together and he was blindfolded, but his mouth was free. To be precise, what was left of his mouth was free. As far as he could feel, he no longer had any lips. His brain began to go through the facts. First, the attack on him was organised when the sun was up, so he had clearly not been kidnapped by vampires. Second, who would want to injure and kidnap him in this way? Perhaps it had been organised by his wife, or his wife's family, or his cousins, or even his friends. He knew better than anyone how many lives he had ruined, but somehow he felt that the attack was related to his work. Third, perhaps FATHER wanted to get rid of him. After all, the old man was known for his hostility towards those who had gained power, and Christopher had become stronger in the last few years. He remembered how he used to have bodyguards, but one day FATHER had asked them to be removed; budget cuts, supposedly. But perhaps it was all part of his plan to destroy the Guild's vice-president.

One of the kidnappers, a young man, began to speak.

'Thunder is here; nature knows that the war is about to begin.'

As he said this, he opened a packet of dry biscuits and popped one in his mouth. The sound of the biscuit being eaten pained the vice-president's ears; after all, he was very hungry, but couldn't say so. Then a second noise was heard, far worse than the first; a bottle of pop had been opened. A loud burp next to Christopher's ear made him jump.

'I bet you want to eat my biscuit and drink my drink,' the boy said. 'Imagine being treated like a God most of your life, and then robbed of simple pleasures. Ooh, it must feel pretty bad.'

A girl chipped in, saying in a happy, juvenile voice, 'Come on, don't tease him. Remember, we are not allowed to torture him emotionally, only physically. Life is so limited sometimes.'

Christopher heard the voice of the second boy again.

'Speaking of limited options, did you guys hear the news? Amazon has put on a limited sale of these new video games for a week, starting Monday.'

The second girl said, 'What the hell? There is always a sale on video games. We live in such a double-standards society. They never put decent discounts on make-up. But for boys, well, there is always a discount.'

The first boy said, 'Come on, these days chicks play video games more than boys.'

The second girl said, 'Well, I know men who wear make-up, but they are not the majority. At least not yet.'

'Shut up!' the girl who had attacked Christopher shouted; she was the leader of the small gang.

They drove for another two hours until finally, the car came to a stop. As they dragged the kidnapped man out of the van, the rain started to fall. As the big drops landed on the poor man's wounded face, he wanted to scream out in pain, but he couldn't, as he had no vocal cords left. He passed out.

When he eventually returned from the land of unconsciousness, he realised his blindfold had been removed. He opened his eyes and saw a grandfather clock with no hands in front of him. It could be any time of the day; if indeed it was still the day that he was attacked.

He was tied to a white wooden chair in the middle of a white room. Everything was white: the walls, the floor, the carpet, the ceiling, the clock, the chandelier, the office desk. Perhaps it was in an attempt to make it appear pure.

Christopher realised that half of his tongue was missing and he could feel the air brushing against his gums. He began to cry in silence.

A few minutes later, the door opened and the girl who attacked him and was in charge of the teenagers entered. She was wearing a long white gown, and was carrying a white suitcase and a white bowl. She walked barefoot towards him and put the suitcase and the bowl on a white table next to Christopher's chair. There was a white spoon in the bowl. She began to eat slowly in front of the captured man's hungry eyes; it was rice pudding with coconut cream on top.

After she had finished, she opened the suitcase and took out a long, thin, sharp knife with a white handle, a wooden globe painted in white, a small white shaving mirror and a small sound recorder, white of course!

She held out the mirror so that Christopher could see his face; his left cheek was badly burnt, and he could see the veins and muscles exposed around his eye. His upper and lower lips had disappeared, and his teeth were shining like an army of pearls. His chin was also destroyed and the flesh burnt. Worst of all, his moustache was gone; the man's pride and glory. His right cheek was less damaged, but nonetheless, the skin had become a black leather-like mass.

The girl returned the mirror to the suitcase and leaned back in the chair.

'If I humble myself in front of you, it's not out of respect. It's just that I want to see how your throat looks from here so that I can cut it better,' she said in a cool, relaxed manner.

Christopher tried to say something, but he failed.

The girl laughed psychopathically and turned on the sound recorder.

'My father was a priest,' she began. 'He told me once that we are all good at many things, but exceptional at one thing and one thing only. You, Christopher, for example, are good at being a jerk. How do I know this?

Well, I read the report on you. Oh yes, we know you better than you know yourself. After all, how can we unmask decent people if we don't know how indecent they are?'

She pushed the knife into her left thumb, and as the blood oozed out, she sucked it away.

'I can't be a vampire yet,' she continued. 'I'm too young, only 16. But I don't mind practising while I'm waiting. If we drink a handful of a person's blood, we can begin to feel their pain and fears. Good memories are not absorbed like that; only the dark, sad images of our lives can be transferred through our blood. That is why every new generation is far more broken than the previous one. Let me feel you, my half-dead prisoner.'

Christopher began to sob, and he was shivering with fear.

'Well, well, well. My little boy is afraid of death. Didn't you used to say to your young hunters, dying for FATHER and humanity is a privilege, not a painful experience? Well, I want to give you that honour and privilege. As you bleed, you become more and more honourable, like my wife-beating, two-faced father. Like my weak, obedient mother. Like my bitch of a sister. Let us all be great in one way and one way only.'

She stood up and opened the wooden globe from the centre. She held its lower part in one hand under his throat and with the other hand held the knife against his throat and made a slicing motion. The blood began to swim freely into the globe.

When the container was full, she poured the blood into Christopher's mouth. She continued killing him by refilling the globe from the dying man's throat. Meanwhile, Christopher, thanks to the blood he drank, began to see and feel his pain and fears in a new light. It was horrible, like being the last man standing on top of a mountain and looking at thousands, even millions of corpses down below. He was sharing the pain that he had caused others.

In his delirium, his heart was screaming in pain and remorse. His soul was no longer blind, and he could see the false light that had been offered to him by FATHER.

In those last moments as he was dying, he realised the beauty of darkness. There was no light to hurt his eyes any more. There was no reason to try to be good, because he knew those who had invented the light had done so not out of kindness, but out of fear of the darkness. He was ready, finally; after years of lying and pretending to be good, he could enter the darkness and overcome his fear. At the hour of death he was complete; he had reached the truth. And it exploded his heart.

Following Christopher's death, the girl closed the globe and put all the items back into the white suitcase. She shut her eyes and dreamt of days of innocence; they were gone once and for all.

She left the white room and went to the yellow room; the room would become white soon enough. At the far end there was a small bath with hot boiling water inside.

Without taking off her blood-stained garments, she lay down inside the tub and, keeping her eyes open, descended to the bottom. The teenage girl had the feeling of sinking majestically in an ocean. As she was going down, the image of the giant bat in Leto's dream was dancing on the surface of the water: people share dreams.

The girl brought her hand out of the hot water and touched the tip of the bat's wing with her finger; Michelangelo's *Creation of Adam* finally made some sense in her mind. God made the perfect man; man created the myth; the myth created wickedness; the wickedness consumed the last hope for a happy life.

*

Jazz was not the kind of music that attracted Adam. However, since he needed to continue his investigations, there was no escape from visiting Louver.

The environment in the club was fairly relaxed. There were some round tables in the venue, and the stage was positioned in the middle of the warm, cosy room. In contrast to a Victorian-style concert hall, there was no power distance between the musician and her audience. Posters were everywhere, and read: *Tonight, Becky's voice will free us.*

Adam and Atakan looked around. The room had capacity for about twenty-five people; ten individuals were already there. Our so-called heroes chose a table directly facing the stage.

Adam put his gym bag down next to the table; Atakan did the same.

'How was the exercise?' uttered a kind, feminine voice.

The men looked over to the next table, where a beautiful woman wearing a light-green suit was sitting. One side of her face was covered by a gold-coloured scarf on which was the image of a red rose with green leaves.

'It was fine. And you are?' Adam said.

'Ash; but you can call me Eve,' said the scientist.

Adam liked Eve's polite but confident manner.

'May I buy you a drink, Eve?' he asked.

She responded with a kind smile, and said, 'Thank you, but I already have one. I hope you enjoy the show.'

She drank some of her margarita.

Adam was fascinated by everything about Eve Ash. Her fingers, the way they touched the sweat of the glass, the way the sweat moistened her finger, the way her lips parted and the margarita flowed into her mouth. And that physical imperfection, that pearl-coloured surface to the face of a beautiful woman who must have been burnt or hurt in the past.

'Where are you, old man?' Atakan asked his mentor.

Adam looked at him and smiled.

'Go and get us some drinks,' he instructed, and the young hunter obliged.

Adam looked at the woman again, and obsessed over the covered part of her face. The ugliness clearly had more stories to offer than the beautiful side; drama is in darkness, tragedy is in light. At one point he felt a desire to rush over to her and remove the scarf so that he could worship the unseen scars. However, before he could execute his uncanny scheme, he realised that more people were entering the club. Something did not make sense; they were coming as friends or families. None of them had the evil stature of a vampire, if indeed they were the un-dead. Was it possible that Cleopatra No. 5 had lied to them?

Atakan returned with two pints of beer.

As he passed one of the glasses to Adam, he said in disappointment, 'I think we have been on a wild goose chase. This place is as ordinary as it could be.'

Adam sighed. 'I'm afraid you're right. Everyone has a drink, and nothing remotely similar to blood. Above all, they are happy. The beasts we hunt are always sad, lonely people; they don't go out, unless they want to drink blood. At least that's what FATHER wrote in the Guild's manifesto.'

Atakan drank some of his beer.

'Should we leave then?' he asked.

'Well, we have come all the way down here, so we should listen to a song or two and then go.'

He took out his phone and looked at his recent call list. Atakan was watching him, waiting for his reaction. But there was no reaction; there was no message for the old man.

'When we leave, I need to call Christopher. If he wants us to continue this useless investigation, he'll need to find some other hunters. I need rest. Recently, I have been feeling far too tired of living.'

Astonished, Atakan asked, 'Are you sure? You used to push an investigation on until it produced some sort of result.'

'When you do the same thing for a long time, you either become that thing or you grow bored. I think I am bored.'

Atakan moved his chair a little so that he could face the old hunter directly.

'I know exactly what you mean,' he said. 'When I was in the army, I felt like a prisoner. Don't listen to TV ads; your social life is crap. The army pays you shite money, and the hazards of the job, well, there are lots of them. And of course, the educated people either study your involvement in war or write psychological books on your behaviour, or they call you a 'baby killer'. The rich people, they don't give a damn about what you do. They have antiques to buy or escorts to date. The worse treatment, however, is from the poor and working-class people. I am their hero; in the tabloids, these morons call me a fighting hero or a defender of democracy. Of course, they put their lazy ass on the sofa and watch TV shows all day long. And the government pays them to do so. These poor people, they don't go to the theatre, not because they haven't got any money, but because they don't have the vision. For them, being alive is the biggest drama they can afford to deal with. And a fighting soldier, or even better a dead young soldier, gives their drama extra bonus.'

Adam announced proudly, 'I've never seen this side of you, son. I'm … I mean, I don't know what to say. Did you see anything in the war that was worse than being a hunter?'

'In my opinion, vampire hunters are pathetic. Soldiers, on the other hand, are just lambs of sacrifice for the angel of death. You know, I disagree when some people say wars are started because of religion. These people have never experienced war and death. I've seen both, I have survived both and I have been emotionally raped by both. When a war begins, all religions are irrelevant. When a war begins, everyone asks themselves one question: how can I live one more second? And the answer is usually pretty bleak: you need to kill the man who wants to kill you in order to own his one extra second.'

'You need to do the same thing in academia,' said Adam, laughing.

Atakan also began to laugh.

At this moment, an old man dressed in a brown jacket went up on stage.

'Ladies and gentlemen,' he said, 'as you know, we are proud to have Miss Becky back with us this evening. She is going to sing for us with her band, The Purple Travellers.'

People clapped following the man's introduction. He raised his hand for silence.

'As is my way, I will tell you a short story and we will then listen to some crazy and tragic songs.'

The entire venue fell into darkness and a purple light was projected onto the man. Getting down from the stage, he opened his hands as he walked around the tables.

'A Rabbi and an Imam once entered a club like ours,' he began. 'They sat at a table, but didn't order anything. The Rabbi said, "I don't drink because the wine isn't kosher." The Imam said, "I don't drink because I am fasting." The Rabbi remarked, "I thought you didn't drink because it's against your religion." The Imam replied, "My naive friend, I have told you many times that my religion is better than yours. Drinking is a sin for those for whom I say it is a sin. You see, I am not God's man on earth; God is my man in heaven."'

The storyteller stood there and looked at his audience.

A young woman asked, 'Why were they in a place like this at all if they didn't want to drink?'

Wiping his forehead with a white handkerchief, he replied, 'Because they wanted to listen to Miss Becky's singing.'

Seconds later, the jazz singer appeared on stage.

Miss Becky was a curvaceous African woman in her late twenties. She had a nervous smile on her lips, and as soon as Adam saw her, he had a feeling that she wasn't really happy about being the centre of attention; ironic, considering she was a singer.

Becky wore similar purple attire to her band. Her earrings were in the shape of Egyptian cats, and her purple lipstick matched her purple shoes. All the members of her band were white men, wearing purple jackets and purple trousers.

She took the microphone between her short fingers and said in a strong, deep voice, 'Good evening, my lovelies. Today, I want to be part of human history. I want you to give birth to your new selves. It is hard to be ourselves; it is far more convenient to be the other person.'

She moved a little closer to her audience and raised her voice.

'I want you to become one entity,' she said.

Everyone in the room held hands with two others; Adam and Atakan did the same.

'Now,' she said, 'I want you to close your eyes and look inside the blackest eyes you can remember. Free your memory of happiness and sadness. I want you to move closer to the source of all feelings. I want you to remember this always: in happiness, our friends will do anything to steal it from us. In sadness, our friends will do nothing to really help us. Loneliness is the price of being right. Loneliness is the price of being right. Loneliness is the price of being right.'

Becky then smashed the microphone by throwing it to the floor, and the band began to play *Strange Fruit*. She sang without a microphone, but was so loud no one would have known.

Adam could see those dead, lynched, bodies she was singing about, swinging in the trees. When she had finished singing the lyrics, she started again from the top. The old hunter was amazed how strong this woman was; her voice, her clenched fists as she punched the air. He wondered if she had become the song she was performing. As he heard the lyrics for the second time, he felt remorse in his heart. He wanted to scream at himself and ask what the point of it all was. The old hunter remembered his fang collection; those vampires were somebody's beloved.

As the song was repeated for a third time, Adam's pain grew deeper and deeper. He wanted to change; he wanted to become that song coming from Becky's gut.

When she finished the song, Adam looked around. Everyone but himself had tears in their eyes and on their cheeks. Adam stood up, and for the first time in his life clapped for something and someone truly beautiful.

He walked towards Becky, but before he reached her, a bullet hit her in the head. In an instant she was turned to ashes. Adam was still in his own world. He saw among the ashes a big red ruby inside the vampire's heart. He dived to the floor and picked it up, and as he did so, the shooting had already begun.

The old man could hear someone shouting his name. He turned around and saw Atakan crawling like a lizard on the floor with the gym bags, coming to his aid.

Adam shouted at Atakan, 'How many vamps have your army eyes counted?'

Atakan shook his head. 'Fourteen, but the killers are not bloodsuckers.'

Adam took a gun out of the bag and looked around. Atakan was right; there were fourteen armed men in dark-green khaki pants and white long-sleeved shirts, all with long black beards. They were firing at the audience, who were turning to ashes. The vampires died with no fight. Adam knew that soon, he and his protégé would be under fire. He saw a man nearby, dressed in white, shooting and shouting words in Arabic.

Atakan crawled over to Adam and said, 'He is saying my leader is greater than God … old man, there is only one way out.'

Adam nodded in agreement and held his gun tight in his hands. He was afraid; these were not harmless vampires, but real psychopaths. Without any strategy or clear thinking, he stood up. As he did so, the man dressed in white aimed his machine gun at a young male vampire lying on the floor. Adam swiftly aimed for the head of the assassin and shot. The bullet entered the left side of his head and came out the other side. The man's blood was a dark, clotted liquid. He put his hand on the wound, and then collapsed dead on the floor.

Atakan screamed, 'Watch out!'

He pushed Adam down on the floor and fired his pistol a few times at the chest of an approaching zombie. From the wounds a dark liquid oozed out, and then the chest exploded. The blood of the terminated dead-walker covered Atakan; the smell was rotten and nauseating.

'Thank you,' shouted the young vampire Adam had saved.

Adam looked at him. The boy was barely 18. He had fair golden hair and gentle blue eyes. Adam put his hand on the boy's shoulder.

'Run, son, run as fast as you can, and take this.'

He took a small pistol from the gym bag and handed it to the boy. As the boy crawled back towards the emergency exit, Adam saw more vampires, wounded or afraid of the men dressed in white. They were all in one corner of the room, being attacked by three zombies. The old hunter jumped to his feet, and as he did so he heard angels singing Puccini's *Madame Butterfly* in his head: *Con onor muore; I die with honour.*

He began to shoot at the men dressed in white while listening to the music playing on the imaginary gramophone in his head. Now he could see the zombies more clearly; they all had savage, cruel brown eyes, and were clones of humanity's worst nightmare. One of them began to shoot at Adam, and a bullet hit the old hunter's right shoulder. He fell down, but ignored the wound and tried to put a new cartridge in his gun. Meanwhile, two other zombies approached him and shot at him with their machine guns. Adam tried to shoot back, but before he could do so, a couple more bullets hit him in the stomach.

As he began crawling in pain across the floor, cursing the day he was conceived, the right side of his face was sliced on a piece of broken glass.

Blood flowed from his face as well as his shoulder and stomach. He was in pain, but before he could think about death, his sins and his daughter, he saw an injured zombie on the ground. He was trying to pick up his weapon to shoot Adam in the head. Adam's gun was inaccessible.

'See you soon, dad,' he said to himself.

The angel of death was about to come and collect what was left of Adam's soul when a bullet hit the neck of the injured zombie. It was the young vampire whom Adam had saved. The saved had returned to save the saviour.

The two other zombies shot at the boy and killed him instantly.

'Bastards, all of you, bastards!' screamed the injured hunter.

Atakan came to his rescue, holding two pistols. He emptied all of his bullets on the two zombies and killed them instantly. He then dived to the floor and reached for the second gym bag.

'This pussycat will keep them away for a while,' he said as he took out a machine gun.

Adam knew that Atakan's attempt to fight the zombies was fruitless, as there were many more pouring into the club. Sooner or later the young hunter would die. Adam crawled over to the dead young vampire, but he had already turned to ashes. Only one thing was left: a light-green wristband, on which was written the word *Peace*.

Adam turned back and tried to ignore the sound of shooting. Blood was oozing from his wounds, and some of the vampires saw it, but they kept running towards the emergency exit or crawling underneath the tables. After all, life has more value than blood.

He turned around and looked at the ceiling; he was waiting for death when an idea crept like darkness into his mind. He grabbed the gym bag that was nearest to him and looked inside. There were a couple of pistols left, which would have no chance against a group of machine guns. There were also the small, purple ball-shaped bombs. He counted them; there were ten. He took a knife out of his pocket and cut the long leather handle of the bag. He felt like he was about to faint. He grabbed a whisky bottle that was lying on the floor, still half full.

'I never liked whisky,' he muttered to himself.

He drank some, and then poured the remainder on his wounds; the pain was severe enough to keep him awake.

He tied the bombs together using the gym bag's handle while talking to himself.

'You know, Leto, I may not be the father of the year, but, darling, you're not the daughter of the year either.'

He then crawled with difficulty towards Atakan. He saw exactly what was happening. Vampire ashes were everywhere. Atakan had killed three or four of the men dressed in white, but there were at least another ten of them left, and more zombies were still entering the club without paying the entrance fee. He held the bombs in his left hand and with his injured right hand pressed the image of the wolf on one of the bombs.

For a second nothing happened, but then the wolf turned red. Adam took a deep breath and cleared his head of all the nonsense that had preoccupied him for such a long time. The images of all these murdered vampires had had a negative effect on his mind that even years of therapy couldn't put right. He gathered all his energy and waved the bombs around his head, then threw them at the zombies. Then he moved behind Atakan and pushed him with all his power to the ground.

'Come on, boy,' he said in a weak voice. 'Cover your pretty bald head.'

Only seconds later, the bombs began to tremble. One of the men dressed in white bent over and picked them up. The shaking stopped. Then, ten small three-headed wolves appeared out of each bomb, growing bigger and bigger, and suddenly, they exploded. The aftermath of the explosion cracked the ceiling and the floor tiles; it was like a volcano had erupted.

The remaining zombies were reduced to pieces of flesh and dark liquid. The final wave of the explosion picked up the two hunters as if they were weightless, and threw them out of one of the windows.

It was all too much for the old man, and he lost consciousness. Atakan stood up, coughing, covered in shards of glass, dust and ashes; minor injuries covered his hands and head. He coughed again and then saw Adam. He quickly took off his shirt and tied it around Adam's stomach wound. He noticed a yellow scarf with a red rose on it flying through the air. He grabbed it and tied it round the old man's right arm. He picked up his mentor, and dragged him as fast as he could towards his car.

As he did so, he muttered to himself, 'Excellent. Other men carry some sexy creature in their arms, I'm carrying a bleeding old man. Oh well, it could have been worse. I could be helping a communication student or an assassinated pope.'

CHAPTER 8

God spare me physical pain and *I'll take care of the moral pain myself.*

Oscar Wilde

Darkness was the religion of psyche. No light could be seen. For a moment, Adam regained consciousness; a moment later, he lost it again. After a few minutes, he opened his eyes and looked at Atakan; the young man was covered in ashes and blood.

Adam opened his mouth, but all he could utter was, 'Leto.'

Atakan didn't look back at him and just kept driving, conquering the heart of darkness.

In his state of hallucination, Adam heard the whispers of the young man. 'Don't die on me. You're the father I have never had. Don't die on me.'

The old hunter asked his own heart painfully, 'Where am I? What is this feeling of displacement? Why so many questions and so few answers?'

The car finally stopped in a dark, narrow alley in front of an old house with a blue door. Atakan got out of the car and knocked on the door five times. After a short while, it opened and a young Japanese woman appeared.

She looked at him with a mixture of hate and love for a moment, and then said, 'I don't date bastards any more.'

Then she closed the door in his face.

Atakan knocked again and the woman reappeared. She looked at him angrily.

'Hey, Ray,' he said. 'Listen, you can call me whatever you like, but you see, my jam doughnut, a friend of mine is wounded and dying, and I can't go to a hospital, and you are the best person in London to help him under the circumstances.'

'Take him to Tartarus. They have a hospital there.'

'I can't. The last time I was there I stole some drugs and got myself into a fight, plus I trust you more.'

As he said this, he tried to put his hand on Ray's waist, but she pushed him away. She went back inside and left the door open. Atakan pulled the bleeding Adam from the car's front seat and took him inside the house.

Atakan glanced at the familiar cult dress shop. It was not his first time there, yet each visit brought his lost boyhood curiosity back to life. There were capes and helmets everywhere, and some comics scattered about. Holding Adam in his arms, he descended to the basement.

Ray was putting on a pair of surgical gloves while chewing some gum. Next to her were an old metal bed and a large suitcase containing surgical equipment. She pointed to the table and ordered Atakan to put Adam on top, then go upstairs to the kitchen, boil as much water as he could and bring it to her. Simple, but vital orders; Ray's strategy to control what was a challenging situation.

Atakan helped the old man onto the table, and as he was about to go upstairs, he turned round and said in a cheeky voice, 'I have so many good memories from that kitchen.'

'Shut up, and move it,' was the only answer he received.

It took him about ten minutes to carry out Ray's orders. When he returned to the basement, she had already removed Adam's shirt and trousers, and he could see that blood was still oozing from his wounds.

'He needs blood, and lots of it.'

Atakan reflected for a moment.

'Just do your best,' he said. 'I'll go to another friend, he works in a hospital. I'll get what we need from him.'

'No need to go anywhere, you moron. I've got all kinds of blood types here; remember, I was a mob doctor until recently, offering my skills to different gangs. What's your friend's blood type?'

'I believe it's B-positive. What do you mean, recently?'

'Three tall bald men brought in a 14-year-old pregnant girl. She had their child in her womb and they wanted me to remove it. Well, I did, and I removed those three big heads as well, with a chainsaw. The mother is safe now, living somewhere away from all of this. Now, my poodle, you too have a bald head. Before I lose it and introduce you to my chainsaw, go to my room. There is a big freezer, and behind the strawberry ice cream there is a white box. Open it. Inside you will find what you are looking for.'

After he left, Ray began to perform the surgery. She washed the wounds on Adam's stomach and shoulder, and removed the bullets. The bullet in his shoulder had penetrated the bone. It took her a few minutes, but in the end she managed to get it out. The bone was fractured, but not badly; it would heal itself in time. She stitched up the wounds and dressed them.

She then began to work on his face; there were only a couple of minor scratches. She took out all of the pieces of glass first and then washed his face with a little Vodka. She realised how pale he had become.

She checked his pulse; it was very weak. She shouted Atakan's name, and the young man ran down the stairs carrying the blood bag.

Ray inserted a needle into Adam's left arm and connected it to the tube. She then connected the tube to the blood bag. Life began to flow.

After a while, she said, 'He is taking the blood now, and he is still alive.'

Atakan moved towards Adam and put his hand on the patient's head.

He bent over and whispered in his ear, 'Hey, father, hey, old man, hey, teacher, hey, friend, do you hear me? We have lost everything a man *can* lose but is not supposed to lose. Stay with me; just stay with me.'

Meanwhile, Adam was dreaming of amber-coloured whales in a bottomless brown ocean on an undiscovered planet, far away from the blessings of civilisation.

*

Adam's recovery was fairly quick, and in less than a week he was able to walk and talk easily with others. Most of the time, he was alone with Atakan, discussing what to do next. His speedy recovery was due to the blood he had received, which was vampire blood; he was ignorant of the fact, since Ray did not divulge that information to him. Over the years she had used it repeatedly, and the outcome was always positive.

On the morning of the sixth day of his recovery, Adam managed to have a serious talk with his young companion. He was sitting up in bed – which was in the shape of a Batmobile – drinking tea. He looked around his small room that was filled with action figures of different comic characters. Atakan was standing next to the bed playing with a small action figure of Two-Face.

'You know, I think he is the most real of people, Two-Face.'

'Do you think he ever got confused between being good and evil?'

Adam moved a little and replied pensively, 'In his case, yes, since the two sides are so distinctive. On the one hand, he was a figure of law; on the other, the symbol of law's shortcomings. But in our case, most of the time we don't know the difference between good and evil. We do not have the luxury to be superheroes or even super villains. We are as ordinary as everyone else. We treat people in ways that we don't like to be treated ourselves. Of course, when we mistreat others, it's our natural born right. But once we are hurt, we don't see it as other people's right. We see them as the embodiment of evil. We call them wicked, abusive and God knows what else.'

Atakan took the blue gem out of his pocket and showed it to Adam.

'There is no saying or map on this,' said the young hunter.

Adam took it and played with it for a while.

'Let's hope that when the second one is found, it helps us to learn what the hell all the fuss is about!' he said.

Atakan shook his head cynically. 'There is no information whatsoever about the second stone.'

Adam gave a faint smile and said in a cheerful voice, 'Come, come now. I know there is.'

'Then tell me.'

'I believe I know the person who possesses that information, and once I have spoken with them, we will know where the second gem is located. He is a gold mine when it comes to information about such matters. I didn't go and see him sooner because I wanted to follow Sarah's clues. Now I need to go to him; I never gave his name to anybody in the Guild.'

Atakan said nothing and just kept playing with the action figures. Adam changed the subject.

'Your friend, she is kind and strong, and she has strange taste in things.'

'She was a final-year medical student. There was a car accident, and her husband, her son, her daughter, they all went up in flames. The only thing that was salvaged was a small Star Wars toy that had belonged to her son. Since then, she has been collecting all these toys and figures, and she makes capes, masks, superhero pants and costumes for a living. As well as the occasional operation on social orphans like us.'

They sat in silence for a while. Adam finished his tea and handed the cup to Atakan.

'What about the bullets that hit me?' he asked.

Atakan took one of the bullets out of his shirt pocket and gave it to Adam.

'I have never seen anything like this before. It is not a typical silver bullet; in fact, it's not even silver. It's copper. Second, the head of the bullet is not a sharp point like a regular one. Look carefully; it is in the shape of a small saw. Now, when a silver bullet hits a vampire's vital organs, he dies instantly; if it doesn't hit a vital organ, it will seriously injure him. This saw-shaped bullet, however, makes things a bit messy. It's more likely that whoever made them wanted to make others suffer more. And I don't think they kill instantly; even if you are hit by one of these little saws in the chest, it will take the bullet a good three or four minutes to reach your heart. Nevertheless, the pain will be severe enough to paralyse you.'

'What about that jazz singer?' asked Adam. 'She died instantly.'

'She must have been hit by a regular silver bullet. Not all of those zombies had this saw-shaped type of bullet. Maybe they were testing them.'

'Testing?' Adam repeated the word softly.

'Exactly. Of course, this brings us to the next issue of why the hell has no one told me about the possibility of coming face-to-face with zombies? I always thought they had vanished after 1945.'

Adam smiled. 'For the same reason that no one told me about them. No one knew they existed, until one day … boom! They appeared out of nowhere.'

'Is there anything else you want me to do?'

Adam lay down on the bed.

'Yes, get me my phone. Go to the contacts and send our location to Rosie. If she calls back, tell her everything you know.'

'Who is she? Your mistress?' asked Atakan.

'No, she's not my mistress. She's FATHER's mistress and secretary at the same time.'

'What? FATHER doesn't like women!' exclaimed the young hunter.

Adam laughed sarcastically. 'That is what he tells you and me, my boy. Now do as I ask.'

Atakan left the room and completed his assignment. Then he went to the kitchen and made some coffee for himself.

He was in the middle of drinking it when Ray's strong voice asked, 'Question, headmaster; what is it that a man and woman can do together and is far more fun than fucking?'

The young man smiled; he put the cup down, turned back and looked at Ray.

'My dear Miss Carol,' he said in a mock posh accent, 'there is nothing better than fornication between a man and a woman.' Then in a sad voice, he said, 'Of course, the ideal is to love and care for each other. You know, to be mature, sit round a table and go through issues and resolve them. Love each other and respect each other as friends and lovers. But let's face it, I've never heard one lover say to another, 'I love you' and truly mean it. Our romantic lives nowadays are nothing but a show; an illusion of what things could and should have been.'

A tear fell from Ray's left eye. She wiped it away.

'I didn't even mean it when I said it to my own husband. And you know what? Even though he died so terribly, I don't feel any remorse or guilt for not loving him, or even for cheating on him.'

Atakan asked sorrowfully, 'Do you love me, or was it just an affair?'

'No, you bald moron, I don't love you.'

'Moses, Jesus and Mohammad be praised! I was so afraid of being loved.'

They looked at each other; she moved near him until their cheeks were almost touching. As they embraced and kissed each other, Atakan could see all those dead vampires and zombies in the jazz club. As his and Ray's bodies became one, he could see those dead soldiers falling down one after another on foreign soil. The tabloids called them heroes, but tabloids are for working-class people; there is nothing brave and poetic about dying. If it's not the end, it's simply a cheap way of travelling to the next world.

*

The woman Adam called FATHER's mistress had Latin ancestry. She was in her early forties and tall, with short black hair; she would pass as being beautiful. She had been with FATHER for over twenty years. The day she came to visit Adam in the cult shop she was wearing a light-yellow jacket and matching skirt. Before she sat down on Adam's bed, the recovering hunter watched how she put her left hand on the back of her skirt and straightened it.

'Greetings from FATHER,' she said.

Adam gave a sarcastic smile and said, '165.'

'Your IQ?'

'I always see things, and most of the time I keep my mouth shut. I told you my IQ level because I know he is not pleased about me still being alive.'

'So?'

'My depression and self-mutilation over the years have affected me pretty badly, but you need to know, FATHER needs to know, that I am far from being an idiot.'

'What do you want?' she asked coldly.

'Blood keeps the vampires alive; information keeps a destroyed man such as myself alive. Those Arab zombies in the club, they were FATHER's babies, weren't they? And you and FATHER knew about the possibility of me finding a gem there. So why on earth was I there? If you wanted me dead, I have been dead for ten years. Death by retirement, that is. Now, what was it all about?'

She smiled at Adam. 'He always told me that he's not afraid of the bloodsuckers. He's afraid of the day you won't feel bad about yourself. He told me, and I quote: "If Adam Helsing began to love himself, that's the day vampires would need to fear true death." And my answer to your question is this: you're right. He knew and I knew about the first gem. As far as we knew, the vampires obviously knew about it too. It is just a feeling, though. We thought that in the process of finding the first gem, you could find out where the other is, if there is another one. The vampires also hoped to learn from your movements. It was all guess work, though. You see, as soon as FATHER created this society of vampire hunters, we heard from our historians and anthropologists about the possibility of a gem or several gems that would help us understand the history of vampires, who they are, how they have come to this world of ours, what their moralities are, if any. At one point we thought there were many gems; then we believed there were only four; another time we were given information that suggested there were seventeen, and so the search went on.'

'And then of course, Sarah Murphy came along with the idea of there being two gems, and she never produced false information, did she?'

Rosie continued. 'And that was when we asked for you. Christopher was against it; he hated you. Although he was in charge due to FATHER's long absence, it was you who knew about most things. I know that FATHER spoke to you about me from the very beginning of our relationship. He trusted you, for whatever reason; I never found out why. Christopher didn't know anything about me. He was always a little cheap potato with grand, useless, impractical ideas and thus was a perfect head of state.'

'Is he dead?'

'He was found two hours after the incident in the club. He was supposed to let you know that we had found the singer and tell you not to go in. FATHER wanted you alive.'

'Please, describe the image of his corpse to me.'

'We don't think it was the vampires. His lips and most of his nose had been burnt with some sort of acid; we couldn't find out what type. His throat had been cut open, and his heart, kidneys, stomach and brain had exploded from the inside, yet there was no trace of a bomb. It was very graphic.'

Adam felt tears well up in his eyes.

'I've suffered so much in my life,' he said, 'and I haven't achieved anything worth mentioning. But hearing that he died so horribly and in pain makes my life mean something. For the first time in years, I feel pleased and happy. These tears you see are tears of joy that I have been saving for my daughter's wedding.'

Rosie was surprised. 'But you and Christopher used to call each other *my friend.*'

'Oh well, whores call their customers baby, darling, my love, and all that means is: *Asshole, pay me.* Now, what does FATHER want from me?'

'He wants you to stay involved in everything, except the finances of the Guild; as you know, FATHER has a great appetite for money. He is all about money, money and of course more money.'

'What about this nonsense with the gems?'

'We have a team of the best researchers. They know their job even better than you, I would say. They said there is only one gem; they are sure of it. There is no clue to there being a second or third or fourth one. Sarah's information must have been partly wrong. For all these years there has only been one gem, we believe. I will get the one you have found from you now to see what is inside it, if anything.'

'Of course,' Adam said, and took it out from beneath his pillow and handed it to her.

'You will get over Christopher's job. As of tomorrow, there is no such thing as a vampire hunter. All contracts are eliminated. They have been a nuisance for a long time now, and they will be replaced by zombies. A garrison of them came to London a week ago, and more will follow over the next few weeks. So, in a few days, when you go to the Guild and into your new office, you will probably be the only human being there who is not dead.'

'Can they be trusted? The zombies, I mean.'

She brought the blue gem in front of Adam's face and looked through it.

'Yes, we trust them, for they seek no money for their actions. They never break their promise, even at the point of death. Now, do we agree?'

He laughed happily. 'We have a deal. I'll be back in the Guild next Monday.'

'Thank you. And FATHER and I pray for your physical health to recover. We can't hope the same for your spiritual health, which is so damaged that no power can fix it.'

When she had left, Atakan entered.

He looked at the new vice-president of the Guild and said, 'Well?'

'Well what?'

'I heard everything,' he said. 'We did all this for nothing.'

'Relax. Help me to stand up.'

Atakan helped Adam get out of bed.

Adam took Atakan's hands in his own and said, 'Walk with me to the garden, if there is one.'

Once outside, Adam leaned back against a large pine tree.

'I told her what she wanted to hear. To be honest, I could sit behind a desk this very afternoon. However, since they want to dissolve the hunters, let them do the dirty work without us. Things are moving so fast. I think war is inevitable. Today's dismissed hunters are tomorrow's heroes. FATHER and his fanatic gang of zombies will be busy with all the paperwork; they may even kill one or two hunters who are brave enough to complain. The Guild thinks there is no other gem because they have given up hope. You and I have only a few days to find the second one.'

Atakan said passionately, 'Listen, I think they are right. I know there is no second gem, I can feel it. If there was, the vampires would have found it by now. If they are so intelligent to hide their organisation from us–'

Adam interrupted him. 'Knowledge is like light: when there is so much of it, you need to cover your eyes so you can see the reality; darkness and ugliness hide beneath the facade of light. The same goes for FATHER. He has searched the world for these gems, but if there is more than one, there is only one person who will know about it. The man I told you about already, a friend of mine. The bastard has aged quite well. We should go and meet him.'

Atakan sighed. 'All right. But what about FATHER? He has trusted you.'

Adam smiled wickedly. 'Well, that's between His Holiness and myself.'

*

Eve Ash was staying at the Radisson Hotel in Leicester Square, London.

She looked at herself in the mirror, touching the injured part of her face. As she gazed mesmerizingly and lustfully at her wounds, she suddenly felt that they were staring back at her, and she shivered in fear. She could hear the wounds seductively whispering her name.

'Please don't do that,' said the gentle voice of the Painter.

Eve turned around and looked at the man. He was sitting on the small red sofa on the other side of the room drinking blood from a crystal goblet. In front of him was a painting he was working on: *Amore*. The picture was the image of doom. Thousands of demons were descending from the white heavens, while a man in a clown clock holding a skull was gazing at them as they approached him.

'Hawk's blood?' she asked.

'No, sheep's blood. It's hard to find hawks these days. Would you like some?' he asked, offering her the goblet.

She shook her head, and then said softly, 'So, so, so...'

'Yes, yes, yes, indeed. A few more days and we shall perform on a new stage. My new painting has already seen the end of everything. All this fuss shall be over soon and a new era will begin. There will be no more obsession with love, death, good and evil. One race shall remain, purified of all humanity and consciousness. Their only concern will be to keep the wealthy alive.'

Eve stood up and went out to the balcony. She looked at the city at night; it was beautiful. The stars were shining, and there was a hint of summer in the breeze, which danced beneath her light-pink dressing gown.

People were laughing and mingling like pointless dots of history. She shook her head, feeling disgust and pity for them. No matter how strong you are, life's difficulties are stronger. No matter how much you love, the beloved hates you. No matter how good you are, life treats you with cruelty.

No matter how dishonest and two-faced you are, life is generous. This life is hell for good people.

Once upon a time, Eve had a simple dream: to do her job and go home to that cosy, familiar sanctuary. In that dream she had total awareness that she would never be able to afford a big house or a first-class holiday; nevertheless, she could always go home, and her beloved family would be there. But tragedy came into her life when she found her husband in that 'home' with her own sister. Life has so many beautiful dreams, yet it offers so few happy realities. No one can be really happy. All our fingers can grasp is the illusion of happiness.

The Painter put his goblet down and joined her on the balcony.

'Is everything all right?' he asked.

She answered with another question. 'You told me once that you are older than life, so tell me, what is happiness?'

'I will tell you a story which is the truth behind being happy. Once upon a time, a devoted religious man was very angry with God because he believed that since God had given him only one hand, he must be hated by the Almighty. This man would go around and constantly curse God, saying, "Oh, God, you're one unkind fellow. I have only one hand and yet all my life I have followed your commands. Why have you done this to me?" And at that very moment a beggar passed by who had no hands and was laughing and dancing, shouting, "Oh, God! I feel great." The one-handed man was impressed by the beggar's optimism towards life, and so he stopped questioning God's decision to give him only one hand. He went over to the beggar and told him about cursing God and how the beggar had taught him a moral lesson. The beggar laughed even harder and said sarcastically, "You fool! I'm not happy or thankful. The thing is, my ass is itching like hell, and guess what? I have no hand to scratch my own ass. So by laughing and dancing I am trying to forget about the damn itch."'

As the Painter finished the story, he went back inside, and Eve followed him. He sat down on the edge of the bed and looked up at her.

'I've seen more mothers sacrificing their children than mothers sacrificing themselves for their children; I've seen more people being destroyed by love than being saved by love. I've seen enough murders, wars, destruction and ugliness to no longer have trust or confidence in beauty. Like the man with no hands, I know that screams of happiness are just a lame way of postponing all the tears and pain. Of course, I am blessed in some ways. I can reach my own ass. A long time ago I used to wake up to the beautiful flapping of bats' wings. I would see a blood-fall as big and strong as the Niagara Falls. And before all of these images of wealth and power, I remember being at peace. But that was another universe, another life. Now I have learned to block that peace. However, I still remember this much: in the old days there was life, even in death.'

Eve sat next to him, put her face against his and whispered, 'Come now, a few more days. You said it yourself.'

'To be honest, I am worried for my young soldiers,' said the leader of vampires.

'Why? They are all adults. They know what to do.'

The Painter embraced Eve.

'We came from the womb of our mothers to this life and then go to another womb: the grave. I have no loved ones left; I am an orphan. There are times when I wake up in distress, sweating; my hands are shaking and I can't breathe. I have these memories of a giant bat. I see God in all His glory; we are both there, God and I. I look around and I see you too; you are naked and you are breathing peacefully. And then it hit me; I have a war to lead, and I need to win it on my own, as I have no brother to help me.'

Eve ran her fingers through his hair.

'I am not a dream; I am here. And we will win,' she said.

'It is the first real battle that I will lead on my own. In the old kingdom, I was the man behind the scenes. I would run things, cause the war or kill a few bloodsuckers. I was good at being a cautious psychopath. But as for winning the war, being a psychopath is just the first step. You need to be scary and screwed up; a politician, or worse, a religious leader. And I'm neither.'

'I know all this, my love. We have been over this again and again. Forget about it for a moment. Listen, I have brought you a book; promise me that you will read it.'

'Okay,' the Painter said reluctantly.

She went over to the wardrobe, picked up her bag and took out a book, which she handed to him. It had a yellow cover, on which was the title, *The Small Book of an Arab Clergyman: How to Pretend to Be Holy and Live the Rich Life of the Sinners.*

'Who's the author?' he asked.

'No one knows. He or she has concealed their identity.'

He opened the book and read the epilogue to himself.

Good life is the fruit of honesty and decency; wrong. To begin with, there is no such thing as honesty. Honesty is in fact the intelligent way of telling a lie. This kind of lie is a difficult one to discover; so idiots would call you an honest person, or even a saint.

In addition, there is no such thing as decency. Being decent means not being hungry. When we are hungry, we would sell our own mother for a bite of a cheap American burger.

Good life is the fruit of stupidity. For example, consider a Muslim Imam. He does not work his entire life, so his brain is free from the troubles of the world. He has every right to be thankful to God. You and I do not have the same right. He is married at the age of 18 to a 16-year-old girl. When he is 28, he is married for the second time to another 16-year-old girl. When he is 38, for the third time he marries, of course to another 16-year-old girl. And as he turns 48, he needs to get married for the fourth time, to a 16-year-old girl. By the time he is 60, he divorces his first wife, and marries another 16-year-old girl. Of course, when he dies (if he does, as God does not kill wicked people as easily as good people), we discover that our little Imam's life has been recognised by most people as sexually decent.

How can one be bad and enjoy life, I ask? It is very, very easy. We can all be a charlatan, a harlot, and put the mask of decency on our faces. Let us consider the issue of love. We can be loved by a man or a woman; as that person who loved us has been kind to us, we need to destroy them. If we were in the East, we could say, 'I destroy the life of the man/woman who loved me because it was God's will (and to hell with what I destroyed).' If we were in the West, we could say, 'I destroyed the life of the man/woman who loved me because it was my choice and right (and to hell with what I destroyed).'

The other way we can enjoy our lives is to be a vampire in the way that the late Master Voltaire suggested: to be a banker. You will have a very good income, and the more you lose other people's money, the higher your bonus will be at the end of the year.

The next way is to be a creator of evil; no, you don't need to be God. Just become a politician; and remember, if you are a politician, you have an army of idiots and morons to vote for you.

A question: how can one be bad in all of these ways and still look good to the public? This seven-headed monster of mine produces the worst gases of all; the virtues that we have been manipulated by for centuries: Castitas, Temperantia, Caritas, Industria, Patientia, Humanitas, Humilitas.

At this point, the Painter closed the book.

'I know the author,' he said. 'He has not changed at all. Once the war has begun, I will go to meet him.'

CHAPTER 9

"Have you considered how you'll bear the separation, and how he'll bear to be quite deserted in the world?"

Emily Brontë

'What took you so long?'

The young man answered in a low-pitched voice, 'The usual romantic conventions; kisses, goodbyes, I will miss you too, etc., etc. Oh well, as long as it works. By the way, old man, are we still going where we planned to go?'

'Yes, drive to the address I gave you last night.'

These long drives to meetings or fights had always provided Adam with a great opportunity to think about every detail of life, from the ancient wars of primitive tribes he had studied as a student, to *Plato's Republic*, a book given to him by his father from the Helsing family library. On the fourteenth page, there was a small smudge that Adam had made when he was just 3 years old, when he touched it with his hands covered in strawberry jam. Beyond that, the book was as good as new. One day Adam decided to wipe away the smudge, but in the process managed (though he never could recall how) to destroy the entire book. This is life in its truest form; something, even a small point, needs to be imperfect. If you want to make everything perfect, you'll damage the whole damn thing.

Their destination was an antique shop; a cheap-looking, good-for-the-middle-class kind of antique shop. In a proper shop of this kind, one would see a 200-year-old Golden Battleship made in Amsterdam. A lady or a gentleman would approach you, explaining the origins of the ship, and add other details to the history of the object so that when you paid thousands of pounds, you would in fact feel that you had bought a piece of history. In Aunt Peggy's antique shop, however, you would simply be buying some cheap china from fifty years ago with not much history; just a second-hand object.

As the two men entered the shop, the young hunter realised that he was looking at some of the cheapest old objects he had ever seen. None of them particularly appealed to him. Ugliness was everywhere. There was an old lady in the shop reading an early edition of *Lady Chatterley's Lover*; love, finally defeated by sex. Long live lust.

'Hello, Mrs Greene. How are you?' he asked her.

'I didn't like you when you were young and I was young and the world was young, and I don't like you now either. Just do what you have come for. He is down there, controlling things from the basement, a pathetic replica of Hades.'

Adam was not offended by her attitude and simply walked to the corner of the shop where a dark brown curtain was hanging, on which was the image of a burning castle. He drew back the curtain, behind which was a closed door.

He looked back at Atakan. 'Are you coming, or should I send you an invitation?'

Atakan followed him, and the two hunters passed through the doorway and into a dark, very small closet.

'Now what? Should we kiss each other until you find the information you want? Don't tell me that the love and kindness we find for each other here is the lesson of our tale,' said the young hunter.

'Shut up,' said Adam. 'We are going down in an elevator.'

He pushed a button in the dark, and the closet/elevator descended like the moralities of a modern hero. The more the hero loses the ethics of his status, the more he plunges into the darkness of a basic life.

They descended for about a minute. Once they reached the basement, they walked into the most theatrical of rooms, spacious and lit by hundreds of candles. It was filled with shelves and shelves of books engulfing two red sofas. On one of the sofas sat an overweight middle-aged man with blonde hair and short, fat fingers. He was wearing a worn-out shabby Venetian clown costume from which dangled green and blue ribbons.

In a strong, deep voice with an Edwardian accent, he said, 'I'm reading a book about the roots of the carnival in Venice. I've dressed accordingly to understand the carnivalesque tradition as well as I can.'

Atakan laughed childishly. 'Surely it would be more interesting to read about a nudist colony.'

Adam gave him a look and said, 'My apologies, sir; he is young.'

The man said, 'You were younger when you came down here for the first time. You were also the saddest man I have ever known. Sit now, Mr Vice-President.'

Both men sat on the second sofa.

'You are very well informed,' Adam said. 'If it was the early days of our friendship, I would be surprised of your knowledge on matters that the majority of people are not aware of.'

'Well, it is in my blood,' Atakan replied. 'I'm always there when something interesting happens. Here in this room I have around 25,000 volumes of books. Among them I am the freest human being, whilst the outside world is enslaved by goods and sports news. One moment I can be in Peru sodomising the missionaries of the eighteenth century, and the next I can be a slave in China, reporting on the progress of the Great Wall. I can be a fossilised bird being studied by Mr Darwin, or I can be Judas, hanging myself from a maple or cedar tree. I can be dead as I live, or I can be alive as I am dead. Time and logic are of a different vintage down here.'

Adam took his jacket off and then, with some difficulty, removed his shirt.

'What do you think about my injuries?' he asked the librarian.

'How very homoerotic. Well, those that you inflicted upon yourself are still as fresh and deep as they were thirty years ago. The ones from your recent battle, well, you know the answer; they have healed too fast due to the vampire blood.'

Adam put his shirt back on.

'I know,' he said. 'In receiving these wounds to my stomach and shoulder, I came across a triangular-shaped sapphire. There were no embellishments, no carvings and no signs of any kind. FATHER believes it is just a gem that the vampires used to own; something with sentimental value. But I think there may be more, or they might at least have more value.'

'I never liked him,' Atakan said. 'That's why I never offered him my services. I have been warned against men like him by the books I have read all my life. What do you want to do with the gems?'

Adam looked him in the eye and said, 'When I was a student, I hated leaving my research unfinished. Now, years later, I am still tormented by a similar feeling. If there is more to this than meets the eye, which I'm sure there is, I want to find it.'

The librarian stood up and touched his short blonde hair.

'What are you going to do when you meet the person who owns the gems? Bribe him into handing them over to you?'

Adam shook his head. 'No, no, I don't have the luxury of being a businessman. I will get what I want and leave no clue that I was there.'

The librarian smiled. 'If you had given me any other answer I would have said you have become like FATHER, pretending to be a decent, pure human being and then stabbing others in the back.'

He took a cigarette out of his baggy trousers and lit it using one of the candles.

'There are many gems and stones in myth and history,' he continued. 'They represent money, power, gods, demons, love, death, friendship, abundance and all sorts of different parallel concepts. Some also suggest a deep personal attachment to crap ideas. However, at some junctures in history there have been certain insane individuals who have done great things. Although totally meaningless deeds, they were great acts, as their creators were trying to make an impression on history. Vampires are such individuals, and Americans too. There are many stories about the bloodsuckers' wealth; some true, and some false. But one thing is clear, they are not from this universe; they have been sent to us by forces of which we are ignorant. Myth tells us that when they came here years ago, they brought with them a red-coloured object. What was that object? What does it do? What does it symbolise? Who brought it here? Where is it now? I have no answer to these questions at the moment. Nonetheless, I feel that this object must be of great sentimental value for the vampires. Why? Because books do not speak much about it. If it was not a sensitive piece of information, every lunatic would have written about it, like they keep writing about our duty towards animal welfare, whatever that means. The only source that I have found on this matter is an ancient myth written in the Egyptian hieroglyphic alphabet that was found on a papyrus in Cairo in 1917. It speaks of two gems. The part about the material of the gems is missing, but we have the section that says together, these two gems form a map, although of what, it does not say.'

'This is all good,' Adam said, 'but where is the second gem?'

The librarian looked at his cigarette, which had turned into a long white tube of ash; he was so engaged with his storytelling that he had forgotten all about smoking. He dropped the cigarette in the ashtray and relaxed back on the sofa.

'I've never had any vampire clients, at least not yet, so I don't know what exactly is going on. However, I know that many have been looking for these gems, and that's how they discovered the first one in the early 1970s in Denmark. I also believe that the second gem is very near here. Even that the location is in this fine land of ours.'

'How do you know?' Adam asked.

He smiled. 'Because I found it, and sold it in exchange for a very rare book on dark magic in the Middle Ages.'

'Who has it now?' Atakan asked impatiently.

'I think a drunk bipolar rabbit has it now.'

'A rabbit?' the young hunter asked in astonishment.

'*The* rabbit?' Adam said. 'God, I hate this job. I know that piece of work all too well. He is the ugliest living thing to have ever been created. I am a saint compared to that psychopath.'

Atakan asked the librarian, 'Why haven't you told anyone this before?'

'For the same reason I have never told anyone about the hierarchy of the vampires; no one has asked me.'

The two hunters stood up to leave; Adam asked Atakan to give him a private moment with his old acquaintance.

As soon as the young hunter left, Adam said, 'I wanted to ask you something in private. What does the word *arc* mean to a vampire?'

The clown looked at Adam admiringly. 'Well done, Professor. You are really getting the hang of things. The vampire's arc is the mythical vehicle in which they travelled to this world of ours about 3,000 years ago. They did not create humanity or affect our biological evolution, they simply sank their teeth into our veins.'

*

Once outside of London, Adam asked Atakan to stop the car on a country road.

'But we are in the middle of nowhere,' the young man protested.

'No, we are in the middle of somewhere. If you don't know the place, it doesn't make it obscure; it just proves your lack of knowledge.'

The young man pulled over and parked the car in the field. They got out of the car and began to walk deeper and deeper into what appeared to be a small forest.

'As soon as the Second World War was over,' Adam began, 'an American investor came to this area; he was a businessman and an artist, and he wanted to create a village. You see, he had both the vision and the narcissistic appetite to do so. He wanted to leave a legacy. He wanted to create a piece of work. Like a painter, you know? But like most painters, he did not see the dangers that live beyond the painting. I once saw a painting from the East. A beautiful maiden had passed away; her body was covered in a white shroud and carried by two angels to heaven. The work was called *Death Carriers*. But I was not interested in the angels; instead, I was fascinated by the dark road that led from earth to heaven – the deceased's road to light was covered in darkness. That is what was beyond the painting. The message? From one home to another there is nothing but pain, death and darkness. And as for our American friend, well, he never finished his village. The village itself was not utopia either. It has been deserted since the 1960s and no one lives there except the rabbit.'

'Why do they call him that?' asked Atakan.

'He was born deformed. He would be perfect for the Hunterian museum.'

Although the forest had initially seemed small, it was growing bigger and darker as they ventured deeper, like the heart of a romantic. The mud stuck to their trousers and shoes, and insects, big and small, ugly and uglier, were crawling inside their clothes.

As they passed beneath a tall, old oak tree, a drop of water hit Atakan's bald head. Darkness was everywhere and there was no sound except the slight movement of branches; *nature still talks in its silence.* Total darkness is the loudest scream of nature; the day it can be heard will be the last day of life for this old earth of ours.

Finally, they reached a short paved road, the high street of the village, or rather what that was left of it. All the houses were empty, sleeping in darkness. Nonetheless, these deserted houses were as soulless as those that still had inhabitants. One empty of a living heart, the other empty of a living soul. The only light was a murky amber colour coming from a shop at the far end of the village. They walked towards the light, and Atakan realised it was not a shop, but a cinema.

Adam stopped.

'Don't go near him, I will deal with it,' Adam instructed. 'He's a bit, you know, rabbitish.'

They entered the cinema. Its interior resembled a neglected family tomb, the cheap sort in which one buries an aunt on their mother's side. The chairs were old, dusty and broken. The projector was on and screening *Beauty and the Beast.*

'You know, Rabbit, I would really like to know how the hell you have electricity here,' Adam said loudly.

A loud grunt came out of the darkness, followed by the sound of heavy footsteps. Atakan noticed a huge figure lurking in the corner, with what appeared to be an unconventional shape. Finally, the nasal voice of the rabbit was heard.

'I have my secrets and you have yours, old hunter.'

Adam put his hand slowly into his jacket pocket and felt his pistol.

'I need the emerald, Rabbit.'

'And I wanted to be a vampire hunter like you, like so many others. But you didn't let me in, because I was ugly.'

Slowly Adam moved towards the figure.

'Come, come now, let us not speak about the past. You have one thing that I need; give it to me and I will hire you as a hunter.'

Rabbit's laughter shook the room.

'They say love makes an ugly man beautiful,' he shouted. 'I had that love, you know, to kill those vampires, but I was robbed of my beauty. And now you're here, talking to me like I'm a fool. I live in a deserted dream, an empty village that was created by my grandfather, and yet I still know what's going on in the outside world. There are so many hunters who were dismissed as recently as two days ago. You have no money for this transaction, and you shall not have the emerald.'

Adam said in a low voice, 'Everybody knows everything about the Guild. Jesus!'

Then there was silence, except the sound of the film playing in the background. The screen was showing a dancing scene, and the ugly beast was holding the beautiful dark-haired peasant girl in his arms. He was looking into her eyes, and at that moment the soprano's voice reached its highest note; this was the moment of love, the moment of life, and above all, the moment of hope.

Suddenly, it was all shattered. The rabbit pulled a gun out of his jacket, but he was too slow and Adam took out his own gun and pulled the trigger. The bullet hit the rabbit in the left side of his chest. He screamed, pointed his gun towards Adam and shot. Adam dived to the floor, and the bullet hit the wall. The rabbit began to run.

Atakan desperately tried to shoot at the running monument of ugliness, but before he could do so, the huge rabbit knocked him to the floor. The two hunters followed him outside.

It was raining now, and the two men saw the rabbit standing in the middle of the village, wounded. The beast knelt down and raised his head towards heaven. At that moment, a small white bunny appeared from nowhere and ran towards the rabbit; he picked the bunny up and held it in his arms. Then, with hands covered in blood, he began to stroke the bunny's head.

Adam turned to Atakan.

'Wait here,' he said. 'I need to do this on my own.'

He walked towards the rabbit, holding his gun tightly in his hand. He was finally where he wanted to be, standing in front of the kneeling rabbit. The rabbit's chest was oozing blood. Even after all these years, Adam was still shocked by the beast's appearance. Its left eye was blind, while its right eye was as big as a man's fist. Its nose was in the shape of a small lime, and its jaw and teeth were deformed. The left side of its body was very thin, while the right side was over-sized. Although there was no symmetry in the rabbit's anatomy, there was in his ugliness.

As the rabbit played with the bunny, he said softly and tenderly, 'I love rain; do you love rain, Adam?'

'I don't know,' said the old man.

'Your gem is in my pocket, and you know what? I am miserable, but at least I know why. You don't even know why you are miserable.'

'You are wrong; I know now,' said Adam as he too knelt on the ground and looked into the rabbit's eyes.

Atakan was standing at a distance, watching the craziness unfold.

Rabbit wiped some blood from his mouth. 'Don't tell me you have redeemed yourself.'

'No, not after all the damage I have done. But I have realised that what I am doing has destroyed life rather than improving it. It has amounted to nothing. In the early days I told myself I would kill to build; later, I said I would kill to feel solace. Then, I killed just to kill. There is no better place to realise how far from the light you are than at the bottom of a well. I am with Joseph now, waiting for a miracle, so we will be brought out of this loneliness. As for you, I did not hire you because of your deformity. You were my brightest student at the university. I wanted you to have a life away from the bloodsuckers. I felt compassionate towards you, and that was a miracle in itself. Now I want a promise from you, a promise that you won't die. I know this is not the first bullet in your chest. Somehow you always manage to survive injuries and cheat death. Promise me, that the next time you see that bald young man, you will use your insanity and beauty to help him. You see, I am thinking of leaving and going to a retreat to find some peace. And yes, I see beauty in you. Somehow your imperfections have made you a perfect living being standing on your own two feet. I have always admired the fact that your alliance was to you.'

Rabbit looked at him in surprise; he brought the bunny near his mouth and kissed it.

'There is a nun … I mean, she used to be a nun. She calls me by my name: Valentine. She thinks I am special. I will go to her so she can take care of my wounds. And you can have the damn gem, if you show me a sign, a sign that you are not my friend, but that you are not my enemy either.'

'What sign?' asked Adam.

Valentine responded with a chuckle. 'A song about a white rabbit.'

Adam put his gun back into its holster and the wounded beast handed him the emerald gem covered in blood. Adam helped him to stand up, and they began to sing *White Rabbit* together in low, sombre voices.

Once they had finished singing, Adam hugged Valentine and whispered in his ear, 'Remember, you promised to help the boy when the time comes for you to help him.'

The old hunter patted him on the shoulder and then walked towards Atakan, but continued straight past him. Atakan, rather confused, began to follow Adam without asking any questions. They left the village and went back to their car.

As they sat in the car, Atakan asked, 'Why didn't you finish him?'

'Why not, indeed. Perhaps I have started to change, without even wanting to. It doesn't feel good or bad, it just feels fresh. I haven't felt like this in a long time. Has he overseen this?'

'Who?' Atakan asked, confused.

'The king or leader of the vampires, of course. Has he seen that I will change or that I have the potential to change? What do you think, Mr Hunter?'

Atakan smiled, and as he did so two sharp vampish fangs shone in the darkness of the car.

'A small bird will drop frozen dead from a bough without ever having felt sorry for itself,' he said.

Adam smiled. 'And I thought you didn't know that.'

Atakan the vampire knocked the old man unconscious.

*

The tired eyes of the old man were opened to another space; he was in a long, dark room, where the only light was coming from a green *abat-jour* at the far end.

The hunter had been put on a big sofa made of mahogany crocodile skin; in front of him was a coffee table that had been made in Sorrento, onto which was carved the image of a beautiful baby girl with blonde curly hair, big green eyes and sharp teeth. Next to the table, the Painter was sitting on a Sherlock armchair. He was smiling at the old hunter, and his perfect ivory-coloured teeth were gazing lustfully at the darkness surrounding them.

'Couldn't we have more light in here?' asked the hunter.

'No, we are saving money. Can't afford the luxury of full-time electricity; we need to pay for so many things. It's crazy. If I had a choice, we would meet in a hotel room; I feel much safer in a posh environment than my own house. A house is where loved ones should be; once they are dead and gone, one is nothing more than a sad, lonely orphan. People tell you to get over it, to move on, but they don't know how it feels. They will know one day, but by then it will be too late. Too late to help any orphan, including me, including you, including all of us.'

Adam touched his bruised face. 'He's got a strong punch.'

The Painter smiled proudly. 'He told me he had no intention of beating you, but you startled the boy. I always hoped that once you found out he had become a vampire, you would approach the topic with more sensitivity.'

Adam shrugged his shoulders.

'I saw the horror in his eyes as vampires were dying in that jazz club. It was like he was mourning for a dying brother or sister. I knew then what he had become. I like to know the outcome; an old academic like me always likes to know the outcome.'

The Painter played with his goatee. 'I am not interested in that; I have a question for you, and that is why you are here.'

He jumped up from his chair and sat down on the sofa next to Adam.

He put his hand on the old hunter's heart, and said, 'Tell me something, Doctor, what is the opposite of war in your opinion?'

'Couldn't you have kidnapped me like you did Christopher, torture me and then ask me your question?'

The Painter jumped up again and began to pace the room; at one point, he vanished, but then reappeared behind the sofa.

'Christopher was a moron, you are not. Have some self-love, Doctor. You were troubled not because of your personal issues, we all have those, but because you never grew up, never matured. You got lost in the webs of trauma. You see, in every person's life there is a moment when they need to leave home. And by home, I don't mean the small flat they have been living in all their lives with their mommies and daddies. No, I mean home as heart. I provided you with a journey to get you away from all this hatred, to free your heart, mind and bones of all that pain. To give you solace before the hour of death arrives.'

The Painter clenched his fists and continued.

'I gave you a chance to win the struggle. In your search for those two gems – and, I might add, I had no idea about the whereabouts of the second one – you found yourself. I sacrificed my own people so that you could go inward to your own emotions, your own fears; gradually, you have realised that killing is not the answer. It is a tool to defend ourselves against psychopaths such as FATHER. In finding the gems, you found Adam Helsing; you are now finally free from the hunter in you. Now you have a choice in your life: to live in peace, or to sleep in peace. You are like Dorothy; she needed to dream of Oz to be able to fall in love with her own backyard. I gave you that dream, and it will bring you back to your human essence. Now, I ask you again, what is the opposite of war?'

In a calm, relaxed voice, Adam said, 'Peace?'

'No,' the Painter whispered gently. 'All of the concepts of human life are affected by the same limitation: duality. God and Satan, good and evil, beauty and ugliness, love and hate, wealth and poverty. Every single concept is in direct opposition with another. There is one concept, however, one reality, that is above the rest, and it is so powerful that even God and nature cannot fight it: war. War is the mother of all stories and art. Those hippies that begged for peace, Lennon who sang for peace, they were all idiots. With peace we create nothing. But because of war we have hope; something we don't need during peace. Peace results in depression, but because of war we have art, music and literature. Because of war, the strong and the wealthy survive. War is like urine; it cleans the whole of humanity of its poisonous members. Peace is just an overrated commercial notion like Christmas, Saint fucking Valentine's Day, Halloween, Easter, etc.'

Adam, still lying on the sofa, closed his eyes.

'You sound like my brother when he was younger,' he said. 'Look what he turned into: the FATHER.'

The Painter simply said, 'I have been aware of that fact for a long time. No one else knows … not among my people, that is. And as for sounding like him, I know that he, and you and I, are all very melodramatic characters. The difference is, he is a businessman and murderer who only thinks about money; you were killing out of a childish thirst to be involved with things. And I … I am an artist. I kill for the art of killing and mayhem. It is very unfortunate for FATHER and I that our paths crossed. It will be our end, and every single one of us will perish in this war. We are an ancient race, and will be replaced by two-faced members of the society. Smile at people and stab them in the heart; this is the morality that rules over our corpses. However, you need to know one thing: I'm not going to be stuck here. I shall go home, in the same arc that brought me to this universe of yours.'

'The emerald gem, what was in it? I never had the chance to look inside it properly.'

'Nothing; however, the gem was in the shape of a coffin. Put it next to the sapphire and it means blue grave or, as we can both guess, the blue cemetery.'

Adam suddenly jumped up from the sofa.

'I know a blue cemetery. It is the local name for an abandoned graveyard near Yorkshire.'

'I know; we are already digging up the whole place to find what I am looking for: a red object.'

Adam shook his head in admiration. 'Good, very good. I will not waste my time by asking about the red object. If you wanted me to know what it is, you would have told me by now. I have a more interesting question to ask: how did you break into Atakan's soul?'

'When that boy came back from the war, he looked exactly as you look now. A hero who had gone on a journey, and came back a new person with the old self left behind. He experienced war on a large scale. The feud between FATHER and me is nothing but child's play compared to that. War has given him new eyes, eyes that can see the depth of the human soul and ask certain questions: What was the worth of my actions? Why do the tabloids call me a hero if I always follow orders and never break any boundaries to do anything positive and heroic for others? If I killed a terrorist, does this mean I posses the superior morality or the superior weapon? He asked these questions of God, nature and other representatives of divine and human strength, but none gave him an answer. He was left on his own like a bastard on a church doorstep in medieval times. It was my vision, not God's, which saved the boy. It was me who gave him a chance to live long enough to find those answers on his own. I turned him into a vampire.

'Now, my dear reformed Doctor, I'll tell you a little vampire secret. When vampires drink the blood of an intelligent form, that is, a human, they absorb all the traumas and dark memories of that living form. So, in a way I am closer to that boy than his mother; I drank his traumas as I sucked the sad life out of him. And I filled that empty vase with immortality, desire, power and, above all, a great sense of adventure. As I was turning your ex-protégé into one of us, your brother went totally insane. He kept losing money through his activities and needed a war to compensate. He began attacking us left, right and centre. Now, if he wanted to fight me in order to kill me, I would be all for it. But to fight me as an excuse to divert attention away from his financial disasters, well, I invented that game long before any of you retarded boys were even born.

'I asked Atakan to come to see me and told him I wanted to destroy FATHER's image once and for all. My spies told me about his new army of zombies. You see, Adam, a zombie understands less than an ass. You can break into their psyche very quickly. FATHER manipulated them deeply, and they all want to kill my kind. They are brainwashed. Yesterday, they hated Jews, Christians, most Muslims, women, rich people and educated people; today, they hate my kind. They want me dead. And I shout from the depth of my lungs, let death come to me. I'm going to put a burning torch up their backsides before kissing this life's ass goodbye. Atakan is my main general now. A long time ago, our chief scientist made a new anti-suncream for people with skin cancer. I pursued her, in my own way, to weaponise that cream and transform it into a potion; a potion that helped Atakan walk in the sunlight.'

'Why don't you go into the light yourself?' Adam asked.

The Painter chuckled. 'My misinformed friend, I don't need the potion. I am the oldest vampire in this universe. I have come from a place where vampires can dance in the light, but by staying in the dark I keep the sense of drama high and mighty.'

'You have given me all the answers I seek but one; what do you want from me?' asked Adam.

The Painter smiled, rubbed his long fingers together and said wickedly, 'You love your daughter. That's the only thing you have truly loved in your life, and she is a fugitive now. You didn't know this, I know. She is a strong person. She has enough rage in her to turn up the volume of the music of war; she will win the battle and survive the blessings of the so-called decent civilisation. Still, she could do with friends like me. I will find her and help her, if she wants me to, to fit against humanity and its horrifying ethics. I have the means to do that; you don't.'

'As you surely know, over the years I have developed a certain hatred for life,' Adam said. 'I have manifested the physical anger on my own body and on the bodies of vampires. A long time ago there were a few women in my life, including Leto's mother. I never cared about them because they had the ability of creating life, and I hate life. And still, that shred of sanity that is left in me cares deeply for my daughter.'

The Painter bowed respectfully, then moved towards the hunter and kissed him on the forehead. He embraced Adam as hard as he could, and they were now cheek to cheek, like lovers.

'May I have the honour of dancing with you?' the Painter asked politely.

The two men danced together to the imaginary waltz in the semi-dark room.

'As the vice-president,' the Painter said, 'you are the only one who can disable the security system in Tartarus. With no security, I need 5 minutes to get to your room and kill all the guards. As the vice-president, you can download the names of all of FATHER's investors in England and Europe. Once I encounter some of these investors, your brother must show his face to save others from my wrath. My dear friend, once FATHER is out there in the light, I shall defeat the evil with evil.'

The two men danced for what felt like hours to Adam, and finally, he fainted from exhaustion.

The Painter kissed his hands and feet, and whispered in his ear, 'Love those who don't love you, and hate those who love you; this is the only way to survive this show of mortal life.'

CHAPTER 10

He could not go out,
I also realised…
He could not plunge into the daylight that streamed at the window.
It was asking too much of his nature.

D H Lawrence

Adam woke up at 5 a.m. on the 1st of August in his own bed, in his own house. The dream of the journey was over; changes had occurred. What was to follow would only be formalities for the transitional soul, the last touch of a master mason on the gravestone of a once potential lover. It was the very first day that he would work in Tartarus as the new vice-president.

He began his day by contradicting his old self; he shaved his face and did not cut his chest with a razor blade. He washed his injured body, and did not masturbate. He looked at the photos of his parents and his daughter, but did not cry. He emptied his closet of the fangs he had collected over the years; he felt free. He buried them in his small garden and prayed, for the first time in forty years, to someone or something. He put on his suit and did not feel out of character. He prepared his German hunting gun for the day; he did not feel violent. He looked at his own reflection in the mirror; he did not feel disgusted. He could see his subconscious. And that was the point: consciousness, subconsciousness and unconsciousness had married each other, the result of which was the new Adam Helsing.

He ate his breakfast of boiled eggs and brown toast, and then went into the living room. He looked at all his books; a long time ago, they were his life companions. He looked proudly at his former gods before they were replaced by one singular deity, the God of Carnage.

He slowly touched the surface of all his books, kissing them one by one. The old friends from university days had been reconciled. Now they could be together, sharing one last dream of youth, love and tenderness.

Before leaving his house, he turned around to look at it one more time. He saw the angel of death; not in the form of an ancient skeleton, but a handsome young man wearing a white cloak and smiling. The angel took a green apple out of his pocket and offered it to the old hunter.

'Welcome, my tired friend,' he said. 'It is over. You will not think about it any more.'

The ringing of the door made the angel fly away temporarily.

Adam picked up his briefcase and left the house as slowly as possible.

As he got in the back seat of the car, he noticed a rather odd smell. The driver turned around and looked at him; he was a zombie.

'Good morning, Mr Helsing. I have been asked to take you to Tartarus.'

Adam nodded his approval, and the car set off.

By 7.30 a.m. the old hunter was in his office. No security check was needed for Mr Vice-President. He opened his briefcase and took out his two most important weapons: a German double-barrelled shotgun, and a memory stick. He entered the password his secretary had given him earlier and began to download all the files on his office computer.

He stayed in his office all day, and told his staff that he would be spending the night there. At 9 p.m., he disabled the security system of the Tartarus, and 5 minutes later heard the sound of gunshots, followed by the hideous screams of zombies. The end of a legend had arrived as vampires emerged and rose to the surface. The true filth of the underworld would cleanse the fake golden surface of the heavens made by the gods, old and new.

*

Atakan was leading a group of vampires, who were about to bring the Painter's vision to reality. Tartarus was dead in such a vision. The former hero of the tabloids, the present demon of the nation, was wearing khaki pants and a simple black T-shirt with a white skull on the front. His army boots were clean and polished.

The entire group of twenty-five vampires was sitting in a bus travelling towards Tartarus. Atakan took a deep breath and looked at Maestro, sitting in the seat next to him.

'I haven't even used any cemetery powder, and yet here you are,' the young vampire said.

The ancient skeleton replied, 'I am in your mind and thus a part of you. Wherever you go, whatever you do, however you live, I shall be with you.'

'Who am I?'

'Day after day, in life and death, I searched for that perfect happy memory which would replace the most tragic memory of my life, but I always failed. That was until you came into my life and chose me as your vision, as the image of eternity in your mind. You saved me, so, as far as I am concerned, you belong to an ancient race of men; you are the anti-hero. One day, when FATHER is dead and the Painter is dead, and I no longer play my violin, you will rule the very earth you walk upon. You will rise above the human beings, animals, demons and gods. You will be a pure being; you will not love, because you are love itself. You will not be strong, for you are strength itself. You will not be beautiful, for you are beauty itself. You will be the man that Aeschylus, Homer, Sophocles, Dumas, Hugo and Voltaire searched for all their lives. You will be perfect, for you will be you.'

Atakan took the Maestro's skull in his hands and said, 'I'm afraid.'

'Of death?'

Atakan shook his head. 'I am afraid of living. I don't have the courage to die, but I don't have the will to live either. This purgatory of life is getting smaller and smaller every day. There are days when I wake up and ask myself why I should live, when so many happy people sleep in cemeteries or are turned into ashes in crematoriums.'

He closed his eyes, and when he opened them, the musician was gone.

Atakan cleared his head of the visions and prophecies and stood up calmly. The young general could not hear any voices; it was like his brain had stopped all sound from penetrating his soul. One of the vampires gave him a microphone and he began to talk, but the microphone was not working. He switched it on and off, but it was as good as dead.

Atakan threw it away and began talking as loudly as he could without it.

'When we reach our destination, the gates will be open. Whatever you do, remember the following: kill and move as fast as possible. Do not drink a zombie's blood, and if a zombie begs you, don't be fooled. He does not want to live for the sake of living. He wants to live so that later, he can kill you and burn any womb that has the ability of creating life. Tartarus is a good distance away from any residential areas, so we don't need to be too quiet. After we have finished our deed, the cleaning team will stick around and burn the damn place.'

A female vampire with bat tattoos covering her face asked, 'What if your friend does not open the gates for us?'

Atakan responded hoarsely, 'The Painter has a vision. If in that vision the gates are open, then in reality they will be open.'

He sat back down before anyone else could ask another question.

They stopped two miles south of Tartarus and walked the rest of the way. As they reached the gates, everybody took their weapons out of their jackets and bags as quietly as possible. Atakan took out a medieval war hammer from a big leather bag, while one of the vampires put a magazine inside an Uzi and handed it to him.

As the security gates were unlocked, they made a clicking noise; the vampires opened them with a gentle push and entered Tartarus.

Once inside, Atakan said softly, 'Remember, there are seventy of them, and I want them all to rot in hell tonight.'

He walked as noiselessly as he could over the green grass and saw the back of a zombie. He instructed his men to stop, and put the Uzi in the back of his pants. He moved closer to the zombie in the darkness of the night. The man heard a twig crack underfoot and turned around swiftly; the vampire-general waved the hammer around his head and struck it against the zombie's skull, causing black liquid to squirt out. The battle for Tartarus had begun.

After the first zombie had fallen under the hammer of the vampire warrior, Atakan turned to his men and said in a satisfied voice, 'Ladies and gentlemen, let us began our *Dance of the Macabre*. Maestro, play the music.'

*

It takes human beings years to create an empire, but only a few morbid moments to destroy it. Tartarus, with all its strength as a building and from the ideals that it represented, was gone in a matter of minutes.

Atakan and his small army of vampires annihilated the zombies, who were quite powerless against the surprise attack. Their nature was to be against such wars; the problem was, they knew how to destroy, but not how to defend. Why? Because they never built anything of any value that was worth defending. Some of FATHER's investors were aware of this, and FATHER, in order to convince them, had put the zombies in charge of Tartarus to prove his personal trust in the former terrorists. But his vision had failed him, unlike the Painter's vision, which had given birth to the destruction of the enemy.

Atakan was waving his weapon about and darting amongst the zombies as they fell to the ground like dry leaves in autumn. Finally, he stopped; he felt there was no need to lead his people further into destruction. They were mightier and stronger than Alexander's army; they would see the job done.

None of the zombies stationed outside the building had survived, and those remaining inside were trying to shield themselves. Atakan pointed to the iron gate of the main building. One of the female vampires moved towards it and put a small bag at its base. The other vampires then did the same. All of the bloodsuckers backed away and Atakan took a detonator out of the back pocket of his trousers. He pressed the pink button in the shape of a lamb on the device, and the bags exploded. The sound of the explosion was minimal, since they were acid bombs, but soon the iron gate began to melt.

Once inside, the vampires talked to the dead by death, killing all the zombies. Not a single one could survive, for it would have been against the will of the vampires.

Adam was sitting in his office drinking whisky. He heard the sound of running feet. He calmly put the glass down on his desk and picked up his shotgun. As the door swung open, two zombies rushed into his room to hide. But before they were able to utter a word, Adam fired the gun twice, and it took one bullet to kill each. He then stood up and emptied the barrels of the gun. Adam put the gun down and finished his whisky.

He walked over to the window and stared out at the dead bodies covering the ground of Tartarus.

As he reflected on the scene of victory, Atakan's familiar voice said, 'It is done, old man.'

'Yes.'

Atakan went to stand next to his master.

'Come, we are going to burn the place. We need to leave.'

Adam turned round and looked at his young companion. He was drenched in zombie blood.

The old hunter said, 'I have two choices: to leave here and live as a new man, or to live and rest in peace as a new man; I will not leave and live. Virgil and Dante are now out of the gates of hell. Virgil has learned more than his student; nevertheless, the master shall stay behind and pay for his years of thoughtless behaviour.'

Atakan shook his head in disapproval and shouted, 'No! I will not let you behave like an idiot. I made a personal promise to the Painter to take care of you and I shall do so.'

Adam smiled faintly and put his hands on Atakan's shoulders.

'Don't be so dramatic. I am too tired from rebirth to learn to walk and talk again. Finish it; set me free from all the exhaustion. You were the best of companions I could have asked for. There is a brown briefcase for you under my desk; inside there is memory stick for the Painter. There are also the names of all my contacts. You will need them, as they will help you in this war. One day you will be in charge of all the vampires, I have seen it already. Your Painter also has seen it.'

He rested his head against Atakan's, and the general's sharp white fangs began to grow. As he bit Adam's jugular vein, the blood flowed free and the old hunter felt warm and sleepy as he fell to the ground.

Once his body hit the floor, Atakan bent over, picked him up in his arms and drank as much of his blood as possible. He then let go of his teacher's body, and without looking back went over to Adam's desk, picked up the brown briefcase and left.

Life was ebbing from Adam swiftly and happily. He opened his eyes and looked up at the ceiling.

'Leto...' he said weakly.

Moments later, Dr Adam Helsing slept.

Within half an hour Tartarus was burning in flames. One painting was finished.

*

At 2 a.m. the morning following the incidents that marked the destruction of the Tartarus, Leto was standing outside an orphanage, a building dating back to the nineteenth century. It had six floors, and the spirits of the unfortunate children that had lived there were still floating around. But Leto's interest was on the ground floor, where there was a massive window through which one could see the outside world.

The window's exact location was in a room shared by four young boys, one of whom was her favourite. He had two red eyes and would not talk; not because he could not, but because he did not want to. This young boy had been adopted several times by various families but had always been returned. And the court would not permit a prostitute like Leto to adopt him. A whore with a golden heart belongs to black-and-white movies, not to a society paralysed by a high sense of self-righteousness.

Leto had been waiting for so long to be with this boy, from court to court, from lawyer to lawyer, but all she had heard was no.

After she killed her client, she had rediscovered her powers. She too had changed. From telling herself that she wanted to be a mother, she had reached a certain practicality that only belonged to Americans. She would now tell herself, *I am a mother and therefore I must save my son.*

Leto was outside her son's jail, playing with a big black rock in her hand. She took a deep breath and started to walk towards the fence between the orphanage and the main road. She climbed the fence and passed the CCTV cameras, showing them the finger of power, and went to stand in front of the ground-floor window.

What Leto saw next made tears fall down her cheek. The boy, her boy, her son, her adoptive soul, her heart, was awake and staring back at her from behind the window. He put his small hands on the glass, and Leto did the same. The boy smiled sweetly and wrote in the condensation on the window, *Mom.*

She showed her son the rock, but he walked away from the window. Leto threw the rock at the window as hard as she could, and as soon as it broke, the screams of the children and the sound of alarms were in air.

By the time the sleepy security guards were out of their beds, Leto and her son had already reached the fence.

'They are coming! Climb up!' she shouted.

The boy showed no emotion, and instead he calmly and in a psychopathic manner walked towards the only guard that was approaching them. Leto was shouting in despair. But as soon as the boy reached the guard, he jumped high enough to be level with his head and then punched him in the face. The boy was strong; he broke the guard's jaw and nose, leaving him unconscious.

He returned to his mother and they climbed the fence together. Then they ran as fast as their legs would carry them and were soon inside the woods. The deeper they ventured, the tighter they held each other's hand.

The sound of the police cars could be heard in the distance.

Leto was worried they were lost. Suddenly, thousands of bats appeared from nowhere. She hugged her son and dived to the ground, but the bats did not attack them and like pilgrims circled a tall shadow. The shadow and bats moved towards the mother and child. It was the Painter.

He bowed to them, and said, 'There is a van waiting for you; let us help each other. I am sorry that I did not bring the Rolls-Royce; it is being serviced.'

He helped them to stand up. Leto was desperate to ask the stranger why he wanted to help her and how he had found them, but she could hear the police cars and preferred to trust the mysterious man rather than the law, since the law and its decency had failed her significantly in the past.

The three of them walked in the darkness, the bats escorting them.

When they reached the van, Leto, the boy and the Painter climbed into the back. The vehicle belonged to those who had killed Sarah Murphy and Christopher, and their leader was waiting for the three of them. Once everyone was in their place, the girl gave the order to drive, and the van moved on.

The teenage girl looked at Leto and asked what her son's name was.

Leto answered, 'Whatever he wants it to be,' and kissed his small head.

As they travelled along the bumpy road, the Painter's head hit the roof of the car a couple of times, and he bent his tall body over as much as possible.

'Do you have your guitar with you?' he asked the teenage girl.

She pushed away the blanket and picked up an old guitar. She began to play it.

'You know what?' she said. 'I think we could all do with a gypsy song to sum everything up.'

She did not sing the song, but read the lyrics of *The Sound of Silence* in the same way that one reads a bedtime fable to one's three imaginary beautiful black-haired daughters.